NOVEL

1

Irina
The
Vampire
Cosmonaut

WRITTEN BY **Keisuke Makino**   ILLUSTRATED BY **KAREI**

As the words left her lips, she didn't even try to hide her fangs. The cafeteria filled with stunned silence. Lev tried to clear the air with a chuckle.

MIKHAIL YASHIN

ROZA PLEVITSKAYA

LEV LEPS

"I'm Irina
Luminesk.
I hate humans.
Don't talk to me.
That's all."

IRINA LUMINESK

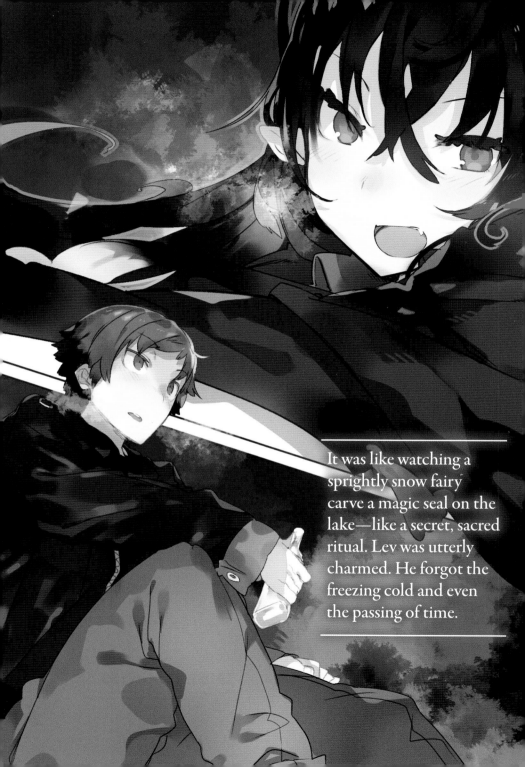

It was like watching a sprightly snow fairy carve a magic seal on the lake—like a secret, sacred ritual. Lev was utterly charmed. He forgot the freezing cold and even the passing of time.

"Sinus Iridum...
Lacus Somniorum...
Palus Somni...
Oceanus
Procellarum..."

Lev prayed with his entire body, fists clenched tight. A deafening roar echoed around them, as if the earth were coming apart. Smoke covered the ground. The rocket shook and slowly rose.

"Fly, damn it, **fly.**"

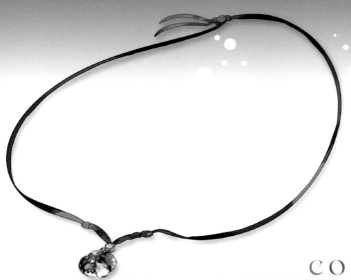

CONTENTS

Луна, Лайка и Носферату

Original Cover & Logo design by Junya Arai + Bay Bridge Studio

Irina

The Vampire Cosmonaut

NOVEL

WRITTEN BY
Keisuke Makino

ILLUSTRATED BY
KAREI

Airship

Seven Seas Entertainment

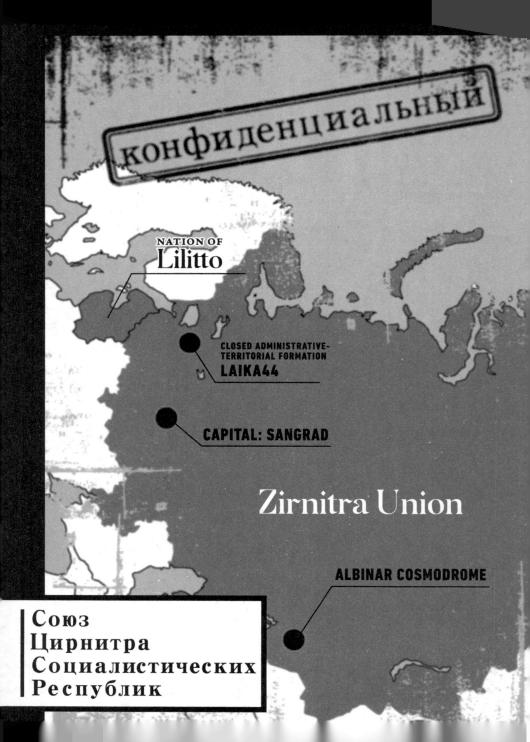

конфиденциальный

NATION OF
Lilitto

CLOSED ADMINISTRATIVE-
TERRITORIAL FORMATION
LAIKA44

CAPITAL: SANGRAD

Zirnitra Union

ALBINAR COSMODROME

Союз
Цирнитра
Социалистических
Республик

Characters　Луна, Лайка и Носферату

■ **LEV LEPS:** 21 years old. Air force private second class. Cosmonaut-candidate reserve.

■ **IRINA LUMINESK:** 17 years old. Vampire. Nosferatu Project test subject.

■ **MIKHAIL YASHIN:** 25 years old. Air force private second class. Top of the class among the cosmonaut candidates.

■ **ROZA PLEVITSKAYA:** 22 years old. Air force private second class. Cosmonaut candidate.

■ **SLAVA KOROVIN:** Rocket development chief.

■ **DR. MOZHAYSKY:** Somatologist. Plant and animal experiment supervisor.

■ **ANYA SIMONYAN:** Irina's data analyst.

■ **LT. GEN. VIKTOR:** Cosmonaut-candidate instructor.

■ **NATALIA:** Dorm matron.

■ **VICE-DIRECTOR SAGALEVICH:** Cosmonaut Training Center vice-director.

■ **FRANZ FELTSMAN:** Hot room training engineer.

■ **FIRST SECRETARY FYODOR GERGIEV:** Supreme Leader of the Union of Zirnitra Socialist Republics.

конфиденциальный

[This story is fictional. All characters, organizations, and names are fictitious and have no relation to existing people.]

TSUKI TO LAICA TO NOSFERATU Vol. 1
by Keisuke MAKINO
© 2016 Keisuke MAKINO
Illustration by KAREI
All rights reserved.
Original Japanese edition published by SHOGAKUKAN.
English translation rights in the United States of America, Canada, the
United Kingdom, Ireland, Australia and New Zealand arranged with
SHOGAKUKAN through Tuttle-Mori Agency, Inc.

Seven Seas press and purchase enquiries can be sent to
Marketing Manager Lianne Sentar at press@gomanga.com.
Information regarding the distribution and purchase of
digital editions is available from Digital Manager CK Russell
at digital@gomanga.com.

Follow Seven Seas Entertainment online at
sevenseasentertainment.com.

TRANSLATION: Hengtee Lim
ADAPTATION: Rebecca Schneidereit
COVER DESIGN: H. Qi
INTERIOR LAYOUT & DESIGN: Clay Gardner
COPY EDITOR: Rebecca Scoble
PROOFREADER: Jade Gardner
LIGHT NOVEL EDITOR: T. Anne
PREPRESS TECHNICIAN: Jules Valera
PRINT MANAGER: Rhiannon Rasmussen-Silverstein
PRODUCTION MANAGER: Lissa Pattillo
EDITOR-IN-CHIEF: Julie Davis
ASSOCIATE PUBLISHER: Adam Arnold
PUBLISHER: Jason DeAngelis

ISBN: 978-1-63858-576-3
Printed in Canada
First Printing: August 2022
10 9 8 7 6 5 4 3 2 1

прелюдия

SCARLET EYES
• ОЧИ АЛЫЙ •

"SINUS IRIDUM..."

On a freezing night of smoky mist, a young woman looked up at the silver full moon from the old castle's snow-covered balcony. There was loneliness in her whispers.

"Lacus Somniorum..."

Dust and grime sullied her long deep-red gown. Her limbs were fragile, and her skin was as white as porcelain. Her fangs clashed with her pretty lips.

"Palus Somni..."

The girl sang the words of the old song with great care, one by one.

"Oceanus Procellarum..."

The wind swept up her black hair, revealing her pointed ears.

"Mare Vaporum..."

The girl unfastened the small jewel around her neck and held it toward the moon. Pure blue light shone in the clear crystal. A green aurora floated into the sky, as if dangling from the moon.

"My wish..."

The girl's bright crimson eyes turned a deep scarlet. The evening breeze took her whispers, and they disappeared over the scorched plains that had once been forest.

She clasped her hands and stared up at the moon. She entrusted it with her fleeting prayer, although very quietly.

INDIGO EYES
• ОЧИ ИНДИГО •

T HE ROOM WAS DECORATED with countless wooden fighter planes. Inside it, a young boy with gray-streaked blond hair sat while his mother tended his bumps and bruises. The child was so enamored with the sky that he'd built wings from cloth and sticks and leaped from the roof of his home. A quick crash landing in an aronia shrub had resulted.

His mother scolded him, her expression as fierce as any monster's.

"Nosferatu swoop in and bite stupid children's necks, you know! Keep up your madness, and *you'll* get bitten!"

"Stop it, Mother." The boy quivered; his hands raced to shield his neck.

The Nosferatu were a feared bloodsucking race in Zirnitran legend. There were many such stories of blood-drinking monsters—the upyr, the nelapsi, the strigoi—in Zirnitran folklore. Barring a few exceptions, none truly existed. All the same, their names alone left many children cowering in fear.

Sipping at zhizni, the boy's father echoed her. "You can give up your dreams about that pilot stuff if vampires leave you shaking in your boots."

"Wh-what difference does that make?!" objected the boy.

"Well, tell me this. What will you do when a Nosferatu comes at you during a flight?"

"I..." The mere thought set the boy's whole being ablaze with fear.

His father laughed. "Scared, aren't you?"

"Am not!" the boy replied, his face bright red. "I eat garlic every day, and I wear a cross around my neck! I'll be fine! If a vampire tries anything weird, I'll shoot them down!"

His mother and father exchanged a glance, then burst into laughter.

"What're you laughing about?! Stop it! When I'm older, and I'm piloting tours of the moon's surface, I'm never taking you guys! Not ever!"

"Tours of the moon's surface?" his mother repeated. "How many decades before *those* happen?"

"Come to think of it, I've heard vampires nest on the far side of the moon," his father added.

"Y-you're fibbing! I'm going to the moon and proving you wrong!" The boy looked up at the full moon floating out past the window. His indigo eyes sparkled in the light. "Just you watch me."

1955 Eastern Calendar (E.C.) —

Ten years after the war that split the world in two, life at last returned to a state of calm. During this peace, two superpowers set their sights on the stars above, a vast and unclaimed domain. Thus began a fierce competition between the Union of Zirnitra Socialist Republics (UZSR) in the east and the United Kingdom of Arnack (UK) in the west.

October 1957 —

The UZSR successfully launched the first man-made satellite in recorded history, Parusnyĭ One. The UK, believing their nation technologically superior, was astounded. Their reaction was dubbed the "Parusnyĭ Shock."

The UZSR subsequently launched Parusnyĭ Two, successfully sending a dog into space. The UK responded with the rushed creation of their own satellite, which exploded two seconds into launch.

September 1959 —

The UZSR's lunar probe landed on the moon, leaving behind a metal cube engraved with the country's name and emblem. Three weeks later, building on the excitement and momentum, the UZSR successfully photographed the far side of the moon, which until then had been completely unseen.

The UZSR's Supreme Leader, empowered by the nation's continuing successes in space, sent the president of the UK a triumphant message: "Our nation's pride is our lunar landing, while *yours* is still hamburgers."

The UK's newspapers announced a battle of survival, and the UK's space development program moved toward history's first-ever manned spaceflight. Initiating Project Hermes, the nation selected seven air force officers dubbed the "Hermes Seven" for the suborbital flight.

September 1960 —

First Secretary Gergiev responded to Project Hermes by implementing the Mechta Project, which would launch a manned rocket into orbit. His orders were clear: "Find a way to send a human into space before the United Kingdom of Arnack does!"

The battlefield was no longer Earth; it was far away in the heavens—the realm of gods. And there could be only one victor.

CHAPTER 1

The Nosferatu and the Zilant

INDIGO EYES
• ОЧИ ИНДИГО •

Private second class lev leps was in free fall at two hundred kilometers per hour. He'd leaped from a plane three thousand meters aboveground. Outstretching his arms and legs, he let the air resistance carry him. His goggles pressed against his face, wind whistled in his ears, and the cold pierced his cotton jacket.

Below him, other cosmonaut candidates' parachutes began to open, blooming like cream-colored flowers above the sweeping fields. The Bolik River's belt-like flow caught Lev's eye as the Earth slowly grew closer.

"Here we go." Lev's freezing fingers pulled his parachute's ripcord. The canopy flew from the bag on his back, its silk catching the air and expanding like an umbrella. Lev's body was yanked upward.

Lev sighed, swaying in the wind. "This is Cosmonaut Lev Leps," he muttered, "returning from space." His voice dissipated into the air, reaching nobody. "Yeah, right."

Imagining the lecture he'd get if his superiors heard him speak such words, Lev frowned and grasped his parachute's steering lines.

Sunset dyed the desolate marshlands red. Once the parachute drills finished, Lev and the other cosmonaut candidates took an air force bus to the Space Research City known as LAIKA44.

LAIKA44, which Lev now called home, was a national secret—a closed administrative-territorial formation, or "closed city." Built only recently—March of 1960—the city was an important base of operations for the Mechta Project. Its population of nine thousand people were all connected to the initiative.

It wasn't on any maps of the UZSR, and it had no registered residents. In fact, although it was named after Laika, a coal-mining town some forty-four kilometers away, there was no connection between the town and the Space Research City. The government had implemented the cover-up to avoid the UK intelligence division's prying eyes.

LAIKA44's residents were tasked with top-secret jobs, and they were strictly forbidden to speak about their work or its location outside the city proper. Breaking those rules would result in an early-morning visit from the Committee for State Security's secret police—known as the Delivery Crew—and a one-way ticket to the mines.

Therefore, although most ordinary Zirnitran citizens were aware of their nation's successful satellite launches, they had no way of knowing the space development program's inner workings. Fierce dedication to secrecy was the Union's traditional method, and it could be summarized in a single sentence: "To fool your enemies, first fool your friends."

Simply reaching LAIKA44 took considerable effort, since the city was veiled in secrecy. The airspace above was a strict no-fly zone, and no trains passed through the region, so access was only possible via automobile.

After leaving the main highways for smaller roads and passing "Dead End Ahead" and "Authorized Personnel Only" signs, as well as the inspection checkpoint, vehicles had to weave through a dense coniferous forest.

Just as visitors felt their sense of direction disappear completely, the walls surrounding LAIKA44 would come into view. There was only one way in and out of the city—a steel gate protected by security guards armed with machine guns and military dogs trained to sniff out strangers.

Arriving at that gate, the cosmonauts disembarked the bus. They showed the guards their IDs and proof of residential permission and passed through.

"Hey! Lev!"

It was cosmonaut instructor Lieutenant General Viktor. His voice was husky from many long years of drinking, and his uniform stretched across his muscular frame. Lt. Gen. Viktor was a hero of the Great War; the medals covering his chest and the scar running down his forehead were proof. Overall, he cut an intimidating figure.

"What can I do for you, Comrade Lt. Gen.?" Lev asked.

Lt. Gen. Viktor's brow furrowed, and he shot Lev a sharp glare. Lev stood at attention, readying himself for abuse. "Report to the Director's Office in the Training Center. The Chief wants to talk to you in person."

"Th-the...Chief?!" The statement was so shocking, it was like an icicle piercing Lev's spine.

"The Chief" was none other than Slava Korovin, First Design Bureau Chief and designer of Parusnyĭ One. He was an individual so important that his very existence—much like LAIKA44's—was a state secret. For fear of assassination at the hands of the United Kingdom of Arnack, the Chief was in hiding; his real name was known only to those who required it. When it was absolutely necessary that a public announcement mention Korovin, he was referred to only as "the chief designer." His anonymity spooked the UK—they claimed the UZSR was concealing a sorcerer.

The Chief seldom called upon LAIKA44's residents, but Lev had heard rumors that some of the twenty cosmonaut candidates would soon be laid off. Could this summons mean the culling process had started early? He was lost in thoughts of bad news.

Viktor's booming voice brought him back to the world. "To the Director's Office!" He patted Lev's shoulder.

"Y-yes, Comrade!"

As Lt. Gen. Viktor lumbered off, the confused Lev found himself surrounded by other cosmonaut candidates.

"What'd you do this time, Lev?"

"Nice knowing you."

"First a reserve and now discharged!"

Lev avoided his fellow candidates' stares and played things down. "Wait, wait. Let's not jump to conclusions."

"Why else would the Chief call you?"

That was a question he couldn't answer. "Well, um, whatever the reason, I'd better go."

Lev had been selected as a cosmonaut candidate that spring. Over the summer, however, he'd been demoted to a reserve in the aftermath of a fiasco. Now, barring some kind of miracle, becoming the first human in space would be impossible.

"As long as I get up there someday," muttered Lev, ever the optimist. "The important thing isn't getting there *first*. It's just getting there."

Still, the situation seemed far from good.

The Cosmonaut Training Center was in LAIKA44's development sector. The rugged three-story building appeared to be the furthest thing imaginable from a spacecraft.

Lev was a nervous wreck. He walked down the corridor, which was decorated with celestial globes, until he reached the Director's Office. Two members of the Committee for State Security's Delivery Crew stood on either side of the thick oak door, watching Lev's every move as their badges glimmered.

"Well, let's do this," Lev whispered to himself, fixing his tie. Knocking on the door, he called, "Candidate Lev Leps reporting!"

The door opened silently, and tobacco smoke wafted from within. Once Lev had taken three steps into the office, a Delivery Crew member followed, shutting the door behind them.

Lev took a deep breath and gulped nervously, peering at the faces awaiting his arrival. Next to Lt. Gen. Viktor was a tall, thin middle-aged man in a lab coat—Dr. Mozhaysky, the biomedical laboratory director. Mozhaysky was well known for his experiments on animals and plants, as well as for sending several dogs into space. His neatly slicked hair shone, and his immaculately groomed kaiser mustache stood at attention.

In the middle of the room, a man who looked to be about sixty sat back in a leather-upholstered chair. It was Korovin. His hair showed traces of white, but his features radiated powerful energy. His strong build and weathered skin didn't suit a civil servant; they were proof of the hard mine labor he'd done after being falsely accused.

Korovin was the shortest man in the room, but his aura was easily the most intimidating. He blew a lungful of cigarette smoke into the air, and his fierce gaze—like that of a lion staring at prey—pierced Lev. "It's been six months now, my little zilant."

"Yes, Comrade Chief." Sweat ran down Lev's back, making him even more uncomfortable.

"As you know, the Mechta Project pushes ever onward. We're developing the technology to achieve our dreams at top speed. We must succeed at human spaceflight, no matter what, and prove to our hamburger-stuffed enemies who is truly superior!"

Perhaps First Secretary Gergiev had reprimanded Korovin following the Mars probe's latest failure. Nonetheless, Korovin was haughty, arrogant, and full of confidence. In any event, Lev was in no position to speak his thoughts; his rank demanded that he listen.

"The Mechta Project must succeed, but success requires that we overcome one major issue," Korovin continued. "You see, we still haven't confirmed that zero-gravity space is safe for humans. Isn't that right, Dr. Mozhaysky?"

Mozhaysky twirled his mustache with a finger. "Our space-travel experiments have seen the successful launch and return of several canines," he replied, his voice cool and calm. "However, we gather information on body-state changes from our telemetric data, and we're aware of mid-flight issues like sickness and vomiting. We've concluded that we cannot handle humans as we've handled dogs."

Korovin stubbed out his cigarette and quickly rose from his chair. "The Committee of Central Government has ordered us to launch a manned ship into space. Immediately after it enters orbit, we're to announce our grand success boldly to the entire world via international broadcast."

"Wha...?" Lev couldn't believe his ears.

Until now, the UZSR government had steadfastly asserted, "Our national space development program will not fail." Only successes were announced, and always *after* confirmation. The failed Mars probe, for example, had been kept confidential; not a word was publicized. Announcing a spaceflight in progress wouldn't just be an exception to the norm—it would be an astonishing left turn.

Lev was still at a loss when Lt. Gen. Viktor replied, "A successful live broadcast from orbit would embarrass the UK's space program—perhaps past the point of recovery. It would be definitive proof of the Zirnitra Union's victory. It risks our nation's dignity, but it's a grand, bold plan."

Korovin clenched his fist and raised it high. "The Committee of Central Government expects the mission to completely succeed! We won't be allowed the slightest miscalculation—neither during orbit nor during reentry! However—and the question must be asked—how will we ensure a safe flight when no human has yet gone to space?"

Space was an unfamiliar domain; no one knew what effect it would have on human brains and bodies. Humans were equipped with higher cognitive abilities than dogs; could they visit outer space without harmful side effects? Could their mental faculties withstand the view of Earth from orbit? Might a terrified pilot do the unthinkable on the tightrope between life and death? Assuming a safe return to Earth, could a space journey cause long-term debilitating side effects? The unanswered questions swirled around the UZSR's development team, creating a mountain of uncertainty.

"If a pilot behaves irrationally or dies mid-flight on national television, that'll leave us at the mercy of the whole world." Korovin frowned. "There's nothing I want less."

Lev felt overwhelmed by the conversation's sheer scope, and

Dr. Mozhaysky's next question caught him off guard. "Lev, you may wonder why our experiments use canines over primates."

"Uh, er...yes." Monkeys and their close primate cousins were certainly more humanlike than dogs.

Mozhaysky twisted his mustache, looking dissatisfied. "They're useless. When you put a primate in a cockpit simulator, they break the switches and rip off the sensors attached to their bodies. Compared to cute, obedient dogs, monkeys are too innately curious. That's the worst kind of developing intelligence. Besides, the fact that we can't communicate with them has proven an issue all its own."

"And if cosmic rays evolved those primates into humans, we'd be out of the frying pan, into the fire!" Korovin cut in. "Comrades, we'd behold the birth of history's first spaceman!"

His joke missed the mark, but everyone in the room laughed along affably all the same.

At this point, Lev still had no idea why Korovin had summoned him. This didn't feel like a conversation that would lead to his dismissal. Did they expect him, a reserve cosmonaut candidate, to secretly stand in for a primate? Would they eventually just claim a reserve was little more than a mannequin?

Korovin seemed to notice Lev's apprehension. He quickly faced the private, meeting his eyes. "Comrade Lev Leps."

"Sir!" Lev readied himself.

Korovin paused before asking, "Do you know of the Nosferatu?"

The sudden question took Lev off guard. He blinked in surprise. "I-I'm sorry. Did you say...?"

"You heard me correctly. The Nosferatu."

"Er... Yes, sir. They're legendary bloodsucking monsters. The term also refers to blood-drinking residents of Lilitto's borders."

"Yes. I'm referring to the latter."

The nation of Lilitto, west of the Zirnitra Union, had been invaded by enemy forces and burned virtually to ash during the Great War. Although the nation had crumbled, the UZSR managed to occupy it, and Lilitto had joined the Union. The Nosferatu lived in Anival Village, deep in the mountains. Most people had long considered them a cursed species.

The government's Unification Policy forbade the Nosferatu from leaving their village. That meant almost nobody in the UZSR had ever seen Nosferatu, even in photographs. Lev was no different. However, as a child, he'd heard countless tales of vampires. They'd left him with an image of the Nosferatu as cold-blooded, coldhearted monsters who sucked the blood of the living in the dead of night.

Korovin's reply confused Lev further. Why were they suddenly talking about vampires? What did the question about Nosferatu have to do with the space program?

Korovin cleared his throat. "Listen carefully. The project I'm about to describe to you is top secret."

"U-understood, sir!" Lev's heart beat faster. Viktor and Mozhaysky peered at him.

Korovin's low, stern voice cut through the discomfiting silence. "Before launching a manned spaceflight, our department will conduct the Nosferatu Project, which will test zero-gravity space's effects on a vampire test subject."

"Huh?"

"Codename N44."

"Erm, yes, sir." The conversation had passed beyond Lev's understanding.

Mozhaysky moved smoothly into an explanation. "Vampires far surpass primates in terms of... Well, we can safely say they're extremely similar to humans. Not just in the composition and construction of their bodies—their blood-analysis data is also no different from a regular human's. In short, they're perfect candidates for experimentation. And they're biologically classified as nonhuman, so if we send one to space, that won't be part of Humanity's Great Work."

"Indeed." Lt. Gen. Viktor nodded. "The first human in space absolutely must be one of our citizens."

Mozhaysky straightened his mustache. "We plan to launch the test subject in two months. The experiment will gather the same data monitored in canines. We'll confirm cockpit safety, measure the effects of cosmic rays and zero gravity, and analyze changes to the test subject upon their return. Should the subject die during the project, we'll behave as if we never conducted the experiment in the first place."

Lev sensed that he was finally grasping the conversation's key points. A vampire was to be sent into space as a human substitute. He felt there was something inhumane about that plan, but he wasn't in a position to weigh in on a state-sanctioned initiative.

Korovin again turned to Lev. "Here are your orders."

"Sir."

"You'll manage the test subject until its launch. Furthermore, you'll take part in its training. You can think of yourself as its supervisor."

Lev's eyes widened with disbelief. "Uh, er... Supervisor?" He felt countless questions rising. The most pressing was simply, *Why me?* "Permission to speak, Chief?"

"Granted."

"Why assign *me* this task?"

"That's not your concern. The decision's been made."

"Understood."

"N44's success is hugely important to the Mechta Project and the dreams of the human race. Will you accept this mission?"

Lev lowered his gaze, hesitant. Korovin had demanded a yes or no answer, but test-subject supervisor was *not* a normal task for a cosmonaut candidate. Lev wondered whether they were assigning him the role out of pity for his rank as a reserve—or was it simply that no technician would accept it?

His reluctance was partly caused by simple fear of vampires. Although Lev was a courageous pilot who generally knew no fear, he still found ghosts, spirits, and monsters unsettling. His parents had instilled such terror in him that he'd wet the bed several times as a child.

Since Lev was a reserve, however, refusing this assignment would just seal his status as a failed cosmonaut candidate. His pilot license would be revoked, and his path to space would be blocked for the rest of his life. He had to avoid that at all costs.

Lev raised his head and met Korovin's gaze. "I'll happily take it on, if you deem me suitable."

Korovin's mouth curled into a satisfied smile. "You're to carry out your duties according to Lt. Gen. Viktor and Dr. Mozhaysky's instructions. The plans are in their hands until launch."

"Understood!"

Viktor patted Lev firmly on the back. "I'll inform the other candidates."

A reserve paired up with a vampire would be in an awkward position among the cosmonaut candidates. Lev broke into a nervous sweat just thinking about it.

"Also, I'm sure you already understand this, but you're to treat the test subject as an object," Viktor told him. "For this particular project, it's imperative that you don't become attached."

"Yes, sir." Lev felt hesitant. *Am I even prepared to handle such a terrifying monster?*

"Follow me, Lev." Mozhaysky nodded at Korovin and then ambled toward the door.

Lev gave a final salute. As he left the room, Korovin called to him. "One last thing. Given that you're a reserve, your current chances of being selected as a cosmonaut are virtually zero."

"Yes, sir." Lev was already well aware of the fact, although it hurt to be told so bluntly.

"Still, I expect great things in your future."

"Huh?"

Korovin's eyes narrowed meaningfully. "Now go, my little zilant."

"Sir!" Saluting Korovin once more, Lev stood at attention, heart aflutter with hope that he might yet have a chance to be a cosmonaut.

The dark colors of evening deepened with each moment as Lev followed Mozhaysky behind the Training Center and through a red pine forest. Just as he got used to the pine resin's cloying scent, the two arrived at a tidy little building not unlike a hospital.

It was a wing of the biomedical laboratory—a facility for raising animal test subjects. There were numerous buildings in LAIKA44 that cosmonaut candidates weren't allowed into; the biomedical lab was one of them.

"The test subject is in the deepest part of this building," Mozhaysky said.

The guard at the lab entrance was protected by iron bars and didn't open the opaque glass doors until Dr. Mozhaysky presented his ID. Lev followed the doctor inside nervously. He felt distinctly like a test subject himself.

The lab was much gloomier than the Training Center. Gray pipes snaked along the walls of the linoleum-floored hallway. Poor ventilation left the air stale, and Lev heard dogs howling somewhere deep within the facility. He followed Mozhaysky farther and farther into the building, passing chambers lined with animal cages.

They finally arrived at a large hexagonal room. In each wall was a thick steel door labeled with a numeral from "I" to "V." In the room's center was a small, box-like chamber; the sign dangling from the door read "Guard Room."

The strange sight of it all sent a shiver down Lev's spine. "What is this place?"

"These are cells for humans," Dr. Mozhaysky said simply.

"W-wait. You're not telling me you've experimented on humans, are you?"

"No, these were only built as contingencies. They haven't been used. This test subject is the first we've kept in them."

"Contingency" or otherwise, the cells' mere existence made Lev shudder.

Suddenly, a furry creature leaped out of the guard room.

"Huh?!" Lev cried. *Was that an escaped beast? A vampire?!*

It turned out to be neither. Lev found himself facing a young woman in a fur coat. She was small, perhaps a head shorter than Lev himself.

The girl's face brightened at the sight of Dr. Mozhaysky. "Supervisor!"

"Nothing out of the ordinary?" he asked.

"Nothing! It's been very quiet." The girl turned to Lev and nodded quickly. "Nice to meet you!"

"Hello," said Lev. "Are you the doctor's daughter?"

"I most certainly am not!" The girl opened her fur jacket to show a white lab coat, flashing her ID. "I'm an Air Force Medical Institute researcher!"

"S-sorry!" Lev ducked his head apologetically.

Mozhaysky began a more formal introduction. "Lev, this is vampire biology specialist Anya Simonyan. She's eighteen, but don't let her age fool you. She's a distinguished, capable young woman."

Anya puffed her chest out proudly.

"Now that I've introduced Anya, Lev, the test subject's in Cell I," Mozhaysky added.

Standing in front of the cell door, Lev imagined the monster that might wait on the other side. The blood-red eyes; the fangs capable of piercing human necks; the dark, elegant garments and bloodstained cape; the skin as pale as the dead. The cosmonaut reserve was silent and full of ice-cold fear.

Mozhaysky, on the other hand, had seen the vampire before. His manner remained entirely cool and collected. "If you'd open the door, please, Anya."

"All right." Anya knocked on the cell door, then said casually, "We're coming in."

Without a hint of hesitation, she turned the key and gripped the door handle. With a start, Lev popped his collar—a precaution to hide his neck, ensuring that whatever was inside the cell wouldn't suddenly jump out to attack him.

With the heavy sound of metal scraping the floor, the door slowly opened. The concrete room inside was dim and cold. There were no windows, and the only source of illumination was the electric light dangling from the ceiling. At the back of the chamber were a toilet and sink. A black-haired girl in a military uniform sat on a coffin against the wall, reading a textbook on orbital mechanics.

Anya pointed at the girl. "That's the test subject."

"Huh?" The figure Lev saw was so unexpected, he couldn't keep his jaw from dropping.

The girl, draped in shadow, stood silently. She turned to Lev, watching him. She was a little more than a head shorter than him, with skin as white as snow. Pointed, elflike ears poked from her hair. Her determined eyes, bordered by long lashes, were a pale and almost listless crimson. Below her thin, neatly shaped nose, fangs no different from a kitten's pointed from her small, pale mouth. The transparent blue jewel dangling from her neck reflected the light above.

"This girl's...a vampire?"

Faced with the sight of the beautiful, seemingly fragile creature—apparently the opposite of a man-eating monster—Lev felt his guard slip. She wasn't so much a vampire as a...princess. There was something cold in her expression, however. Her appearance was human, but Lev felt an invisible wall around her that said, "Keep out."

"The test subject's name is Irina Luminesk," Mozhaysky said. He thrust a new ID card toward Lev. The rank on it read, "Private second class, Air Force."

"Is this her official rank?" Lev asked.

"No. It was only issued to accommodate the test subject's life here, so it can access city facilities. Life without that status would be terribly inconvenient."

Lev took a closer look at the ID. The listed address wasn't the biomedical lab cell but the cosmonaut candidate dormitory.

The girl's age was listed as twenty-one, though she looked considerably younger. Lev knew the ID was fake, but he still paused, wondering whether aging differed between humans and vampires.

Deciding that a proper introduction was in order, Lev stepped toward Irina, rolling up his shoulders slightly for protection.

"I'm Lev Leps, private second class. I've been appointed your supervisor." He swallowed his fears, thrusting his hand out with a smile.

Irina, however, made no move to shake Lev's hand; instead, she stared intently at him. Her pointed gaze left him flustered. Lev didn't have sisters. Since graduating junior high, he'd lived mainly in male-dominated environments like the military. There were a few female cosmonaut candidates, as well as female engineers and technicians, but Lev wasn't particularly comfortable talking with them. His experience with women his age was practically zero.

"Er...it's, uh...nice to...meet you," Lev stammered, chuckling nervously.

Wilting under Irina's gaze, he pulled his hand back. He completely understood her rejecting his handshake. Not only had Irina been imprisoned, but she was also now a test subject in a project that could end in death. She had no reason to be friendly.

"This is for you, Lev," Mozhaysky said, handing him a sheet of paper. "These are the four rules for N44's supervision. Please read them as written, loudly enough for the test subject to hear."

"Understood." Lev did as he was told and read from the paper. "One—complete all required training and examinations without failure until the test launch."

"Each day, you'll be informed of your assignments," Mozhaysky explained. "Based on the results of the examination at Sangrad, the test subject's an exceptional specimen as capable as the current cosmonaut candidates. And there have been no reports of the test subject biting examiners or inspectors, so in that respect, there's no cause for concern."

The dim light above Irina's head buzzed.

"Next, please," said Mozhaysky.

"Two—take every precaution to ensure LAIKA44 residents are unaware of the test subject's true nature." Lev was reluctant to call the girl "the test subject."

"Only a limited number of people are aware that the specimen is a vampire," Mozhaysky elaborated. "Perhaps a hundred total, including technical officers and the state commission. As far as anyone else is concerned, the test subject's merely another private second class."

"It's all right for us to go walk around the city, then?" Lev asked.

Mozhaysky nodded. "This vampire's no different from the canines we raise for experiments. We walk them and play with them to ensure they're mentally stable."

The doctor's words shocked Lev; he stole a glance at Irina. Her expression remained cold, however, as if she wasn't concerned in the slightest by Mozhaysky comparing her to a dog.

"Three—the test subject cannot be allowed to escape. In the event of an escape attempt, the test subject will be...executed." Lev felt suddenly despondent.

"That rule prevents information leaks. In the event of an escape, you too can expect punishment and imprisonment, Lev." Mozhaysky's cold tone confirmed that this was no mere threat.

Without question, trying to run away would only result in Irina's death. Lev wasn't sure whether she was aware of the UZSR's ruthless ways, so he felt it was best to warn her. He turned to Irina. "Please don't do anything stupid. Even if you escape LAIKA44, the Delivery Crew will chase you to the ends of the earth."

Irina heaved an annoyed sigh, her fangs flashing for an instant. "I won't run away."

It was the first time he'd heard her clear, bright voice; it touched his heart. Like her appearance, Irina's voice was no different from a human's, Lev realized.

"Please continue, Lev," Mozhaysky prodded.

Lev read the last rule. "Four—the supervisor will live in the cell...next to...the test subject?" His blood ran cold as he finished the sentence. "W-wait," he stammered. "Does that mean I'll live... here?"

"Indeed," said Mozhaysky. "While you were dropping from the sky by parachute, the Delivery Crew moved your belongings from the dormitory to Cell II."

Lev was completely lost for words.

"Think of it as an upgrade," Mozhaysky added. "You've gone from a shared dorm to a private room with its own bathroom."

"Uh, about that..."

"Relax, Lev. Your quarters are furnished with a bed, not a coffin. The shower's in Cell V, by the way."

Before Lev had any chance to reply one way or the other, Mozhaysky took his hand and passed him a bunch of keys. Lev laughed. There was nothing else he could do; refusing the instructions would end his time in LAIKA44.

"Well, Lev, my duties here are complete," said Mozhaysky. "I've left the rest to Anya."

Without any further ado, the doctor turned to leave.

"Er, excuse me, Doctor...but what do you mean by 'complete'?"

Mozhaysky looked at Lev. "My core responsibilities pertain to the Mechta Project. As you know, our experimental launches of flora and fauna are ongoing. At any rate, enjoy your new quarters."

With one firm pull on his mustache, Mozhaysky was gone in a flash.

Anya walked to Lev. "Don't worry. The doctor's put his full faith in me!"

The researcher looked so young that it was difficult to trust her completely. Regardless, she was all Lev had. "I'll be counting on you, Anya. These orders came very suddenly. I'm basically in the dark about everything I'm supposed to do here."

"Well, all the training and everyday stuff is yours to deal with," Anya replied. "My responsibilities are purely data based. I gather medical information and check the test subject's numbers. I spend most of my time in the lab."

So he and Irina would usually work as a pair. Lev scratched the back of his head. He was a bit nervous about whether he was really up to this.

"Moving along," Anya continued, "Irinyan will—"

"Wait." Irina's voice was pointed.

Anya cut herself off. "Something wrong?"

"What do you mean, 'Irinyan'?"

"It's a term of endearment."

"I don't need your endearments."

As Irina rejected her new nickname point-blank, Anya spun toward Lev. "Why don't you call her Irinyan too?"

Why would you ask me to do that when she literally just rebuffed you? Lev wondered. Irina turned her icy gaze on him. "Er…"

Whether or not they called the vampire "Irinyan," one thing was certain—they couldn't keep calling her a "test subject" when they were out in LAIKA44. "Private Second Class Luminesk" wouldn't work either, since cosmonaut candidates never addressed each other by rank.

Lev thought about it. "To avoid leaking your identity to the public, I think we should refer to each other as regular cosmonaut candidates do. I'll call you Irina, and you can call me Lev," he suggested, half expecting Irina to dismiss him outright.

Irina stared at him, silent. Under the light, her eyes were a mysterious scarlet. Her beauty defied human intelligence, and it sent a shiver down Lev's spine. His breath caught in his throat, and his body froze.

"Uh, um…" he stuttered.

"Fine," said the vampire. "Call me Irina, then."

The words seemed to lift the spell on Lev. He sighed in relief.

"I wouldn't ordinarily allow a mere human to use my given name," Irina went on, "but I guess we don't have a choice."

Lev gulped, shocked by her sheer arrogance. If Irina had been wearing a beautiful dress instead of a military uniform, she could have easily passed for an aristocrat. Apparently, Lev's first impression of her as a princess—vampire princess or otherwise—wasn't far off the mark. Still, at least she'd allowed this concession.

"And I should call you Lev, right?" Irina asked.

"Yes, Irina."

Anya took the opportunity to leap in between them. "Glad we figured that out, Irinyan!"

Anya's entirely obnoxious comment made even the stone-faced Irina gape. "Are y-you…?"

"I'll just call you what I want, since I'm not a cosmonaut candidate. Please, call me Anya!"

Anya's unflappable, blasé tone seemed to sap Irina's will to argue. The vampire merely shrugged. "Whatever."

"All right!" said Anya with a satisfied nod. Instantly, her expression changed to a serious researcher's. "While you're here, Irinyan, you'll follow the same training regimen as other cosmonaut candidates. But your daily schedule will start from sundown, given your weakness to sunlight."

"If she's accidentally hit by sunlight, will she be all right?" asked Lev. In all the legends he knew, sunshine was a vampire's weak point and turned them to ash.

"The sun irritates vampires' skin with a burning sensation. But if Irinyan here hides under a parasol or something, she can go out during the daytime without issue. Isn't that right, Irinyan?"

"It is." Irina's cold reply hinted that she didn't appreciate the question.

Anya either didn't notice or didn't care. "Irinyan's also weak to high temperatures, so she's prone to a condition similar to heatstroke," she went on. "The temperature levels leaving the atmosphere will be extra dangerous for her. If she can withstand the temperature, though, then it'll be no problem for humans."

"I see." Lev understood the logic, but he just couldn't adjust to talking about the experiments right in front of Irina. Unlike a dog, she understood everything they were saying.

Irina let out an annoyed sigh. "Vampires also surpass humans in a number of ways, Anya. I assume you, as a so-called *specialist*, know how?"

"But of course!" Anya turned toward Lev. "Vampires have two particularly special traits," she said, holding up two fingers. "Night vision enabling them to see clearly in the dark, and cold resistance that means they're perfectly fine in subzero temperatures—even wearing light clothing."

Those traits, she added, made vampires well suited to northern regions where winters were long and daylight was in short supply.

"Now you understand, Lev," said Irina, her voice clear and her gaze proud. Lev sensed that it was important to her to express that vampires were equal—if not superior—to their human counterparts.

"Lev, please take Irinyan for her dinner," said Anya. "You can eat in the dormitory cafeteria. I suspect the candidates will be there already, so please be sure to introduce them."

"Dinner?" But Irina was a vampire. Would she be drinking blood? Lev glanced at her mouth, but it was closed tightly, and there were no fangs in sight.

"What?" the nonplussed Irina asked him.

"Nothing." Lev turned away from her glare back to Anya. "I don't have to prepare her meal, do I?"

"No. Irinyan was assigned the same meals as all the other candidates. For data-analysis purposes, we need her to consume the same food as the rest of you," Anya explained.

"Oh. All right." Lev patted his chest gently in relief.

Irina walked straight up to him. "You thought I'd be drinking blood, didn't you?"

"Wha...?!" His flustered face showed that she was right on the mark.

"Just what exactly do you think I am?"

The quiet but swelling rage in Irina's voice rattled Lev. "Er... what do you mean, 'what'?"

Her lips curled, revealing her fangs. "You thought I was just another lowly bloodsucker like a leech or mosquito, didn't you?"

"No, no!"

"You assume I'm a monster that sucks blood in the dead of night!"

"This is all a misunderstanding! But, er...I'm not clear. Have you *ever* sucked blood?"

"I... Well..." Irina put a hand to her mouth. She suddenly seemed embarrassed.

Lev was stunned. "No way. You haven't? Never?"

"I-I have. A long time ago," Irina mumbled nearly inaudibly. She lowered her gaze.

Anya raised her hand. "Ah! That was the ritual, wasn't it? The traditional initiation on a vampire's tenth birthday, when they bite a goat's neck!"

"Grr..." Irina glared at Anya and then turned to Lev. "That was the one time I drank the blood of the living. I didn't have a choice. It wasn't just me, though—everyone else does the same."

"So, you're a vampire, but you don't really drink any blood?"

"There's a reason for that ritual, historically," Anya interjected, her "researcher" face on. "Vampires draw blood directly from mucus membranes—for instance, the underside of the tongue or the stomach—and transform it into nourishment. When you drank that goat's blood, Irinyan, didn't it energize you?"

Irina nodded reluctantly. "Yes. But that doesn't mean vampires are just senseless monsters like most people think."

"So, you biting someone, like in the legends... That's never going to happen?" Lev asked.

Irina's eyes filled with contempt at his question. "Of course not. If I let filthy human blood into my body, I'd only taint my own blood."

Irina had made her point crystal clear. Not only did she despise being considered a monster, but humankind also repulsed her. Bearing the brunt of her emotions left Lev remorseful. After all, humanity had pushed the vampires to the country's borders and involved them in a war. Perhaps Irina's parents had raised her on stories of barbaric humans, the same way Lev was brought up on tales of monstrous vampires.

Irina's past, however, had nothing to do with space development. Lev was worried about how best to bring up the subject of her training. Since Irina was female, a test subject, and another species entirely, she was as mysterious to him as the cosmos itself.

Lev mulled it over for a second. No matter how deeply he thought, an answer refused to present itself. At the same time, he knew one thing for sure—to make his dream of visiting space a reality, he had to fulfill his duties.

Making up his mind, Lev addressed Irina in as bright a voice as he could. "Well, I don't know about you, but I'm starving. Shall we get some food?"

"Fine."

He'd expected resistance, but Irina was unexpectedly open to the idea. She took the cap beside her coffin and put it on. With her pointed ears hidden by the hat's earflaps, she looked even more human.

"Anya, would you like to come along?"

Anya shook her head. "I have other things to see to. Make sure you come back immediately after eating, though. Irinyan's already exhausted from traveling from Sangrad, and your day-night schedules are going to flip around. Starting tomorrow, you'll go to sleep at nine in the morning and wake up at five in the evening. So eat up, and make sure you're well rested. Take care!"

With that, Anya saw them out of the isolated cell block.

As the sun sank, the walled town faded into purple twilight. Lev and Irina passed through the forest, with its strong sap scent, onto a path lined with streetlamps and white birches.

"Look, this isn't because I think you'll run away, but I need you to walk beside me," Lev said.

Irina had moved a subtle but apparent distance ahead of Lev. He wasn't about to put a collar on her, but he still had to make sure she stayed within eyeshot.

"Fine. I refuse to be led by a human, though, so side by side is as good as you'll get."

Irina's hostility was clear and immediate, but in a way, Lev felt it was better for her to be open about it. The alternative—Irina hiding her true beliefs behind a friendly facade—was terrifying.

The citizens they passed turned to look at Irina, and the tobacconist even checked his glasses. None seemed scared in the slightest—rather, they looked enraptured. They had no way of knowing Irina was a vampire, so they were simply drawn to her beauty.

Lev had to wonder just how these people would change if they knew what the girl really was. He was full of nervous hesitation as he and Irina headed toward the residential sector's dormitories.

LAIKA44 was divided into two parts—a development sector and a residential sector. Cosmonaut candidates spent most of their time on the city's outskirts in the development sector.

In addition to the Training Center, the sector was dotted with special training facilities, laboratories for engineers and technicians, and buildings of various sizes. At the city's edge, an eighty-meter-tall parachute training facility doubled as a watchtower.

The development sector surrounded the residential sector; the latter contained a school, hospital, library, marketplace, nightlife district, and several similar housing complexes. To make up for the secrecy of the residents' duties, the residential sector was fully equipped with luxuries, including rare appliances like televisions, washing machines, and refrigerators. LAIKA44 was large enough to fit even a soccer field and theater, as well as a man-made lake that, when frozen, could be used for ice skating. The city also contained bomb shelters to accommodate the possibility of discovery by the UK.

Not a single word passed between Lev and Irina; the pair entered the residential sector in silence. A church steeple stretched above the line of rooftops. Its solemn architecture—a golden cross standing upon a blue domed roof—stood out among the buildings.

"Oh," muttered Lev, stopping as he realized something.

"What?" Irina looked at him, puzzled.

Lev felt uncomfortable stating what had crossed his mind. "If we don't go past the church, we'll have to go the long way to the dormitory. But..."

Before he finished his sentence, Irina's cold gaze settled upon him. "And you thought to mention it because you're worried I'm weak to crucifixes?"

Lev felt like he'd stepped on a landmine. "You're saying...you aren't?"

Irina shook her head. "The church used to spread all kinds of lies to entrench their authority."

"Crosses don't affect you, then?"

"Not in the slightest."

Before Lev could say another word, Irina stepped close to him. She licked one of her fangs, locking her arrogant gaze on the reserve. He gasped, backing away. He'd felt pressured by Korovin, but Irina intimidated him in a completely different way. Something about her aura chilled him from the inside out.

"Lev," Irina said.

"Y-yes...?" He felt frozen.

Her eyes reddened as twilight fell upon them. "It'd be a real pain to have to correct every little thing you're scared about. So, here and now, you're going to tell me everything you think you know about vampires."

Irina's face was close enough that Lev felt her breath. He blanched, flustered. "F-fine, fine! But...a little space, please?"

"What're you so scared of? I'm not going to bite."

"Y-you're awfully close," he stammered.

Lev's body warmed, and he worried that he was blushing. Truthfully, he wasn't frightened—he was simply awestruck to be near such a beautiful young woman.

Irina, however, didn't realize this. "Fine, I'll give you some room." She stepped backward, crossing her arms and looking up at him. "This is good, right? Go on, then. Spit it out."

"Er...sure. Things I know about vampires. Uh..." Still shaken, Lev tried to calm his nerves. He searched his memory for myths and rumors he'd heard. "Vampires bite people's necks and suck blood with their sharp, prickly tongues."

"Prickly tongues...?" Irina poked her tongue out. There were no prickles—just a clean, pink tongue.

"That's false, then," Lev acknowledged.

"Next?"

"They can make someone a vampire by sucking their blood. Uh...is that false too?"

"Utterly ridiculous. Next."

"Vampires can't enter someone's home without first being invited inside."

"Would *you* waltz into someone's house uninvited?"

"I... Well, no. No, I wouldn't."

Irina's lips twisted. She was clearly unimpressed. "Anything else?"

"If you spread shells and seeds on the ground, vampires can't help counting them."

"Uh, why?"

"Er...beats me."

"Next."

"You dislike garlic."

"Just the smell."

Lev had made so many awful faux pas, he almost couldn't bear it. But if he didn't want to put his foot in his mouth in the future, he had to get his facts straight. So, although it felt awful, he pushed on. "Vampires transform into bats, wolves, mist, that kind of thing."

"Are you making fun of me now?"

"Vampires won't die unless you run a stake through their heart and cut off their head."

Irina's expression suddenly grew dark and somber. "Don't be stupid. One of those is more than enough."

"Yeah, of course. I...I'm sorry," Lev replied, regretting how insensitive he must've looked.

"Humans are the worst, making up things like immortality."

"Hm?"

Irina's eyes left Lev's face; she looked up at the night sky, which was filling with stars. "We're born like anybody else," she muttered, as if to herself, "and we die like anybody else too."

Turning to look at Irina, Lev saw sadness flash across her scarlet eyes. "What do you mean?"

Irina merely shook her head. "Nothing. Anyhow, when vampires are injured, we feel pain. We get sick too."

Lev was still curious about her prior comment; he felt as if something else was lingering there. Before he could respond, however, Irina said, "Next." She seemed to be urging him onward.

Thus, Lev went back to putting his foot in his mouth. "Vampires are afraid of running water and the sea."

"Not at all."

"Silver hurts you."

"I've used silver cutlery."

"Mirrors! Vampires don't—"

"We have reflections."

"Shadows! Vampires—"

Irina pointed downward at the shadow cast by the streetlamp above. "Do you doubt your own eyes?"

"Oh..."

She released a tired sigh.

"I'm sorry. Really, I am." Lev hung his head apologetically. "I was stupid to just believe those old legends I was told. I'll be more careful."

"You're surprisingly honest and humble for a human," Irina replied.

"Huh?" Raising his head, Lev saw a surprised look on her face. "Well, it was my fault I bought the lies."

"Yes, but it wasn't you who lied in the first place." Irina looked up at the church's cross. "In the sixteenth century, when the Black Death was at its worst, the church treated vampires as though we were the source of the illness. If they made us the cause, people wouldn't blame their own god."

Most so-called legends about vampires were created around that time, Irina explained, and rumors linked to the Black Death were the reason vampires were called a cursed species. That, in turn, led to vampire hunting.

"So, it's not just your fault." Irina turned away from the church and looked at Lev. "You believed those stories because the church spread lies about vampires' unique characteristics and because of the films and stories based on those rumors."

Though Irina had forgiven his mistakes, Lev's heart hurt to think of the horrible things humans had done due to the same misinformation. He looked at Irina with pity.

The vampire girl gazed forward, as if avoiding his eyes. "Take me to the cafeteria."

They passed the stone-paved church square, and the sounds of a choir and pipe organ wafted out from the evening prayer service. Irina pressed her lips tight, as though she didn't even want to breathe the air there. The square was usually a peaceful place where flocks of pigeons gathered and picked at breadcrumbs. But now Lev realized that, for Irina, the church square symbolized things she couldn't easily forgive. He hurried past it.

Once they'd gone by the square, the quiet Irina pointed curiously toward the roadside. In a grassy corner, bouquets of carnations surrounded a statue of a rocket. In the rocket's open window was a small bronze dog.

"What's that?" Irina asked. "The plaque says 'Parusnyĭ.' Does it commemorate something?"

"Ah, that..." For an instant, Lev was at a loss for how to respond. He knew there was no point hiding the truth, however, so he told it. "It's a monument to dogs lost on their journeys to space."

As a rule, the Zirnitra Union announced successes and hid failures. So, for every dog the nation declared a successful space-flight passenger, many, many more were sacrificed for the cause.

In 1957, for example, the UZSR successfully launched Parusnyĭ Two with a dog named Maly aboard. The nation did publicize Parusnyĭ Two's journey through space; however, they didn't reveal that, in reality, Maly had stopped breathing as the ship breached the atmosphere. The heat shield and cooling systems hadn't worked, and the temperature quickly caused Maly to die of heatstroke. Only select people connected to the space development program knew the truth. There was no way Irina, who'd lived her life in the mountains, could've known about Maly.

Irina gloomily stared at the monument, then she walked up to it. Standing before the statue, she put a hand to her chest and bowed. Lev watched her silhouette, lost in a silent prayer. A dark question flashed through his mind—was Irina destined for a similar fate?

"No, not just her," he whispered, shaking his head clear of the thought. "We're all risking our lives."

The manned spaceflight project was built on the sweat and tears of thousands of engineers, and its progress relied on its failures. Before he'd been demoted to reserve, Lev and the other cosmonaut candidates had gone to a rocket pad to watch technicians launch a dog into space. The thought of seeing the first steps of a journey into the cosmos had thrilled Lev. The rocket, however, exploded mere moments into launch, disintegrating completely into ashes and dust. For the cosmonauts, it was like seeing hell before their very eyes. The shock broke their hearts; some were unable to even eat for a while afterward.

Space travel was a bold, grandiose dream, and every technological step was a struggle. Success alone was the height of difficulty. Even when a rocket made it past the atmosphere into space, a small orbital deviation could send it into the depths of darkness or turn it into a literal fireball when it reentered the atmosphere to return to Earth. Truthfully, the success rate of the UZSR's launches was fifty-fifty at best.

Even knowing that all those risks existed, however, Lev and the other candidates continued training. And the girl who now stood before him had been brought to LAIKA44 as a test subject to help safeguard them.

"But why her...?" Lev whispered into the evening air.

Was it because the vampire population was already small, and no others had passed the screening process? He thought about asking Irina but then stopped himself.

"You're to treat the test subject as an object."

Lt. Gen Viktor had given that emotionless order, but the others had been thinking the same thing. The decision wasn't cold-hearted; it was based on the hard-learned lesson of Maly's death.

Maly had been an adorable, happy-go-lucky canine test subject picked up specifically for experimentation. The development team had loved the dog. Many even shed tearful goodbyes when it came time for Parusnyĭ Two's launch months later, knowing that their current technology wouldn't allow a return trip. Mozhaysky, the launch supervisor, had given Maly water right up until the launch. He seemed as if he never wanted to say goodbye. Even Korovin and First Secretary Gergiev had mourned Maly's tragic death.

Since then, test subjects were no longer "comrades." Instead, a line was drawn, and they became objects. *Am I better off treating Irina the same way?* Lev wondered. *As an object?*

"No, I just can't do it," he concluded after some thought.

Limiting emotional attachment was supposed to maintain morale, and Lev's main responsibility as Irina's supervisor was to "complete all required training and examinations without failure until the test launch." Unlike a dog, however, Irina understood human speech. On top of that, she didn't think highly of humans in general. Treating her like an object would encourage her to grow even more antagonistic. If worse came to worst, she might refuse training entirely or flee. Coddling her was out of the question, but Lev still needed to forge a basic working relationship. If he alone treated her like a person, then should the launch end in failure, he alone would feel whatever sadness that caused.

He'd draw a line at treating Irina like an object, but he wouldn't get closer than necessary. That was all there was to it.

Lev turned to look at Irina. She'd finished praying, and now she stared at the night sky. Whatever expression was on her face at that moment was invisible from where he stood.

When he finished his work, Korovin notified the Delivery Crew and headed behind the Training Center to the waiting black car—his private vehicle. Korovin wasn't stationed within LAIKA44, since he was often busy with duties and government meetings that kept him moving from place to place.

Seeing Korovin off, Lt. Gen. Viktor asked, "Why Lev, Chief?"

"That was the decision." Korovin brushed off the question.

Viktor's brow furrowed, and he pressed further. "Are you giving him a chance to clear his name? You know the man he struck was Chief Graudyn's son."

Behind the incident that had caused Lev's demotion to reserve was the shadow of the Fourth Design Bureau Chief, head rocket-engine designer Boris Graudyn. He and Korovin were both hugely important leaders in the UZSR's space development program, and they shared something of a twisted past.

Twenty years earlier, fueled by envy of Korovin's skill, the ambitious Graudyn had attributed fabricated traitorous statements to Korovin, sending the innocent man to the mines. Korovin eventually regained his position; however, Graudyn was never charged for his crimes. Sentencing him to the mines would only have slowed rocket-engine development. It was more convenient for the UZSR to instead erase the incident entirely.

Graudyn's son had also risen to a powerful position; he'd now resided in LAIKA44 for six months as technical development head, and he was an utter tyrant.

"Isn't this against your better judgment, Chief? Whatever Lev's reasons for striking a superior officer, he breached military regulations."

Given Korovin's potential grudge against Graudyn, Viktor logically had a point. Korovin didn't answer, however. Instead, he silently took out a cigarette.

Viktor's muscular chest puffed up with frustration. "Chief!"

"The first time we gathered the cosmonaut candidates to show them the Mechta's cabin was June of this year."

"I'm sorry. What?"

Korovin held his cigarette between his fingers, his gaze distant as he continued. "When it was young Lev's turn to step into the cabin, he took off his cap and gave a respectful nod. He even went so far as to take off his shoes. I've worked with many military personnel and technicians in my time, but none showed my brainchild the respect Lev did that day. He strikes me as unlikely to get riled up about differences between races, countries, and species."

"That's why you chose him?"

"I believe that thinking of the world as one will become more and more important for future generations." Korovin took a deep drag of his cigarette, savoring fond thoughts of outer space. "However," he muttered, "I do worry that there are some who'd clip my little zilant's wings."

The UZSR's space development program had one serious flaw. Since no unified aeronautical space bureau existed, the program's design bureau chiefs competed fiercely. While the cosmonaut candidates chased romantic ideals and long-held dreams, other space development personnel sneakily sought glory and prestige, all too happy to employ subterfuge, conspiracy, and whatever other means were necessary. The true enemy existed not in the UK but within the UZSR itself.

Viktor lowered his voice. "You suspect foul play?"

"No. But it's best to stay on your toes all the same." His expression somber, Korovin raised an eyebrow, glancing at the Delivery Crew standing at attention nearby.

The cafeteria was on the dormitory's first floor. The cosmonaut candidates had finished their dinners and were abuzz with chatter about the new test subject.

"It won't, like, just bite us out of nowhere, will it?"

"Anyone want to bet Lev's already a vampire?"

The candidates were sharing rumors and stories about vampires that they'd heard growing up; a few even had garlic from the kitchen by their sides.

At the center of the conversation were the two most elite cosmonaut candidates. One was Mikhail Yashin, a handsome, elegant young man from a good family; he was top of the class. The other was Roza Plevitskaya, an ace pilot known as the White Rose of Sangrad. She was as graceful as a rose, and so pretty she might've been an actress or model if she weren't a cosmonaut candidate. Mikhail and Roza were well respected, and other candidates were naturally drawn to them.

"What do you think, Mikhail?" one candidate asked.

"Beats me. It is what it is, right?" Mikhail brushed off the question without too much thought.

Roza didn't join the conversation with any real enthusiasm either. She and Mikhail sat back and listened, although they had thoughts of their own.

"And this is the cafeteria." Lev opened the door, and he and Irina entered.

The new arrivals drew the candidates' attention, and their

gossip stopped instantly. Just as quickly as they fell silent, the cosmonaut candidates found themselves suddenly confused.

"Hey, Lev," someone asked, "where's the test subject?"

Lev pointed to Irina, expressionless by his side. "This is her."

"Huh?"

"This is her," he repeated.

The candidates were bewildered. They'd expected a terrifying vampire, but she didn't match their vision at all—the difference was entirely too stark.

"She looks human, though!"

"I mean...her skin and eyes are kind of vampiric."

"Does she have fangs?"

As the candidates focused on her, Irina's expression never changed. She simply observed the people staring, taking in everything. Some were curious, some taken by her beauty, and some afraid to catch her gaze. Among the many reactions, Mikhail looked her straight in the eye, while Roza's lips curled in blatant hatred.

"Go on, Irina," said Lev. "Introduce yourself to everyone."

Irina was confused. "Really?"

"Yes. And take off your cap. No need to hide who you are here."

Irina reluctantly removed her hat, and her pointy ears poked out from her black hair.

"I'm Irina Luminesk." As the words left her lips, she didn't even try to hide her fangs. Her icy voice echoed around the room, bringing the murmurs to a standstill. "I hate humans. Don't talk to me. That's all."

The cafeteria filled with stunned silence.

Lev tried to clear the air with a chuckle. "Heh heh... She's got a bit of an attitude. So, uh...be friendly, all right? Come on, Irina. This way."

As Lev and Irina began to head to the counter, Roza broke the silence. "Is she really going to drink blood in here?"

Irina flinched. "What did you just say?"

Lev rushed between the two, waving his hands to let Roza know that she had it all wrong. "Whoa, whoa! Irina's been assigned the same meals as the rest of us. Didn't Lt. Gen. Viktor tell you anything?"

Roza shrugged. "He just said a vampire was coming. Also said we didn't have to know more than necessary."

It was true that the candidates didn't need to be fully briefed. As far as they were concerned, Irina was a test subject being used merely to gather data, no different from a dog. But without clarification, the candidates would hold on to their mistaken beliefs, and they'd all be on edge if they thought a monster was lurking around the dormitory. That said, repeating the same explanations over and over would get old fast. It was in everyone's best interest, Lev decided, that he give the candidates a rundown on vampires.

"Could I have your attention for just a moment, everybody?" he called.

He explained that vampires were fine with crosses and all the other truths he'd just learned himself. The candidates swapped intrigued glances—and sometimes gasped in surprise—as Lev turned their understanding of vampires upside down.

"Basically," Lev concluded, "Irina's not all that different from the rest of us. And you'll just raise suspicions if you're too obviously wary when you see her in town. Please treat her like everybody else." Most of the candidates nodded at Lev's reasoning.

However, Roza wasn't completely satisfied. She put a finger to her jaw. "You say 'treat her like everybody else,' but she isn't—"

Before Roza could finish, Mikhail rose to his feet, applauding. The loud clapping cut her off. "Welcome to the front lines of space development!" Mikhail exclaimed.

"What...?" His sudden greeting startled Irina.

Lev had known Mikhail long enough to understand that this was just like him. Mikhail knew how to attract attention, and his confidence let him get away with this kind of hammy gesture, for better or worse. Really, Lev had to hand it to him.

Smiling, Mikhail turned to the other candidates. "This girl's sacrificing herself for the sake of our success! She deserves a welcome! A toast!"

The words rubbed Lev the wrong way. It was true that every test subject sacrificed something for the space program, and Mikhail's welcome *was* a perfect example of how the higher-ups expected the cosmonaut candidates to treat Irina. But despite that, Mikhail's wording was tactless. Just from looking at Irina, Lev knew he himself could never be so coldhearted. Still, as long as he kept a clear line between candidate and test subject and didn't leak anything confidential, he'd be fine.

Mikhail ran a hand through his hair and pointed to the counter. "Help yourselves."

"Uh, yeah," Lev replied. "All right."

As he and Irina walked to the counter, Lev noticed that Roza's hateful gaze never left the vampire girl. Was she jealous of Irina's beauty? Did she hate vampires? Was it both? Lev didn't know.

At the counter, Natalia—the dorm matron—greeted Irina with a warm smile. Whether she'd heard Irina's self-introduction or not, she'd decided to approach the young vampire with kindness. "Good evening. I'm Natalia, and I look after everyone here at the dormitory."

Natalia was the very picture of a farmer's daughter in her simple scarf and round glasses. "My, aren't you cute!" she added. "Let me know right away if Lev gets fresh with you, all right?"

"I'll do no such thing!" Lev protested.

"If you touch me, I'll bite you," warned Irina.

"I just *said* I won't."

Natalia put Irina's meal on a tray and pushed it toward her. "I'm not sure whether it's what you're used to, but here's today's dinner."

The main meal consisted of soup full of sauerkraut, rye bread with salmon roe, and a fried mincemeat cutlet. Nutritionists had devised the meal plan to maintain an ideal body type.

"You're underweight, Irina, so you get a special chocolate treat with your dinner!"

Irina tilted her head at the block of chocolate on her tray. "Choco...late?" Since chocolate wasn't available outside cities, she wasn't familiar with it.

"It's sweet and delicious," Natalia explained, "and quite difficult to find in many towns."

Irina stared at the chocolate as though it were a rare import.

"And I've been told you drink milk," Natalia added.

"That's right."

The idea of vampires drinking milk was so strange to Lev that he turned to Irina, asking, "You like milk?"

"Cow's milk and goat's milk are vampires' main sources of sustenance."

"That's...unexpected."

"Animal milk is made of blood."

"Huh?"

"You can even think of it as a blood substitute."

"Uh, I see." Lev wished he hadn't asked. He had a feeling he'd remember that fact the next time he saw milk or ice cream.

Lev and Irina took their seats and were given shots of zhizni. In the Zirnitra Union, zhizni was the people's drink. It was the go-to choice whenever there was reason to toast—even when toasting a vampire.

Naturally, Mikhail took the lead. "To Irina! Cheers!"

"Cheers!"

The candidates raised their glasses high and drank them in a single gulp. Lev did the same as all the others, but Irina left hers untouched.

Feeling the dubious looks of the candidates around them, Lev gave Irina a gentle push. "Not even a little sip?"

"I don't need it," she replied. Ignoring the toast entirely, she sipped her soup with a spoon.

"You can't handle alcohol?"

Irina picked up her shot of zhizni. Without so much as a word, she poured it into Lev's empty glass.

"Uh…"

"I don't know how the rules work for you humans," Irina said, "but back home, you aren't allowed to drink till you're twenty years old."

"Huh?"

"I'm seventeen." She was dead serious.

"Wha…? Seventeen? But doesn't your ID say you're twenty-one?"

"I was told it'd be more convenient if I was considered an adult."

Lev *had* thought that Irina looked young when they first met. Still, he was shocked to discover that she was even younger than Anya.

He laughed awkwardly and did his best to brush off the unexpected discovery. "Well, heh, I guess it's only proper that we, uh… follow the rules, then."

After the toast, the candidates filtered out of the cafeteria one by one, leaving Lev and Irina by themselves. Irina ate silently, making no attempt to talk; the clinking of their cutlery echoed through the empty cafeteria.

Lev stole glances at Irina while he ate. She looked at the roe on her bread curiously, consuming it one tiny egg at a time. As she bit into each egg, it gently popped in her mouth. Lev was so entranced by the sight that he didn't even taste the cutlet he'd been given, although that was usually the highlight of the meal.

Silence. *Pop.* Silence. *Pop. Pop.* Silence.

After taking her time slowly eating each and every bite of roe, Irina turned her attention to the chocolate. She bit into it with some trepidation, then chewed carefully, as though trying to fully comprehend what she'd just put in her mouth.

Lev knew he'd decided not to talk with Irina more than necessary, but his need to maintain a professional distance was clashing with his desire to simply chat with her. His curiosity was getting the better of him.

He gulped down the zhizni in his shot glass. He had a feeling it'd be a tough two months.

SCARLET EYES
• ОЧИ АЛЫЙ •

SO THIS WAS WHO she'd be spending the next two months with. As Irina rolled a piece of chocolate along the tip of her tongue, she stole a glance at him. *Lev.* She was at least relieved to know her supervisor wasn't the abusive type.

She thought back to the tests and physical examinations she'd endured at Sangrad. The memories filled her with humiliation and rage. Her examiners had worn thick gloves and gas masks and looked at her with contempt. They'd fired their questions off rapidly, like machine-gun bullets; answering had sickened her. None of them had said anything to her outright, but their attitudes made it clear how they felt about Irina's "cursed species."

Lev, however, was entirely different. He'd even offered a handshake when they first met—and with a gloveless hand, no less.

That had been a strange moment for Irina, since Lev was the first human who'd been friendly. Hadn't he been frightened of her? What was going through his mind? Was he simply following orders from an arrogant higher-up?

As Irina continued to observe him, Lev became aware of her gaze. His slightly red face softened. "Something wrong?" he asked, tipsy.

"It's nothing." She couldn't admit that she was thinking about him, so she looked away, lifting her glass of milk.

She reminded herself to keep her guard up and not show any sign of weakness. Lev might seem friendly, but she wasn't about to underestimate him. Not him, not Anya, and not Natalia. All it would take was an order from the top, and any of them could transform in an instant.

A vampire means next to nothing to them, she thought. *Just like those dogs who died in their experiments.* If she didn't listen, they wouldn't hesitate to resort to violence. They'd run a stake through her heart, cut off her head, and call it an execution.

Still, she just had to endure for two months. Irina put her cup back on the table, wiping milk from her lips with a finger. *Just two months, and then I'll be free.*

CHAPTER 2

The Path to Becoming a Cosmonaut

INDIGO EYES
• ОЧИ ИНДИГО •

IT WAS THE FIRST DAY of training. Lev awoke in his cramped, cold, and dank solitary chamber. He tugged on his tracksuit and went to Irina's cell. The door was locked, and there was no sign of attempted escape. Lev wasn't sure what he'd do if Irina refused to leave her coffin, but he swallowed his worry and knocked on the door.

"It's Lev," he said. "You there?"

A cold, toneless reply drifted from the cell. "Come in."

Lev opened the door and found Irina sitting on her coffin. She wore a white tank top, and a jewel hung from her neck. She didn't seem the slightest bit chilly—probably due to her species' cold resistance.

When they'd first met, Lev had realized Irina was slim, but that was even clearer now. She wasn't a child, but she wasn't fully grown yet either—her body was still maturing. She looked fragile, like fresh snow; it seemed like she might crumble at the slightest touch. Anybody would've worried about whether such a delicate frame could handle the relentless training ahead.

The previous evening, after seeing Irina to her cell, Lev had received a training itinerary from Lt. Gen. Viktor. It was absolutely packed. Even Lev—who was used to special training—felt that the schedule was pushing it. Irina only had two months to prepare, but if she was injured, a launch would be out of the question. It was his responsibility, Lev realized, to ensure she wasn't pushed too hard.

"Well, let's get to it," he said.

Irina rose obediently from her coffin, grabbing her cap. She turned to leave, her necklace swinging from her neck.

Lev stopped her. "Take the pendant off."

"It isn't allowed?"

"It's not against the rules, but it'll be a hassle putting it on and taking it off all the time."

Irina was silent for a moment. She put a worried hand to the necklace, seeming unsure of what to do. Lev second-guessed himself; perhaps Irina took the jewel with her wherever she went. Maybe it was precious to her. He didn't know much about women's clothes or accessories; he always wore his uniform, and he didn't own any jewelry besides his watch. He looked a bit more closely at the blue gem that shone from Irina's chest.

"That's a beautiful, transparent blue," he said. "What kind of stone is it?"

Irina's hand hid the jewel from him. "Quit staring. Your eyes will taint it."

"Huh? Taint it?" Lev was perplexed.

"I just need to take it off, right?"

As if she had no other choice, Irina removed the necklace. Placing it carefully inside her coffin, she shut the casket lid tight. Lev could tell from each action that the jewel meant a lot to her.

She brushed her hair from her shoulders and put on her cap. "What're we doing today, anyway?"

"Um..." Lev pulled out the daily itinerary. "The schedule changes every day, but it'll basically look like this."

SESSION 1: 1700 HOURS

Fitness training

Physical examination

Meal

SESSION 2: 2200 HOURS

Special-equipment training

Study

Meal

SESSION 3: 0200 HOURS

Strength/endurance training

Parachute-descent training

SESSION 4: SUNRISE

Meal

Free time (showers permitted)

Lights out

"Before I became your supervisor, I was already a cosmonaut candidate," he told Irina. "So I won't just keep an eye on you; we'll train together."

Irina nodded begrudgingly. "I see," she said. "Well, whatever."

Lev was relieved that she hadn't objected. "During study time, you'll learn about rocket engineering and orbital mechanics," he continued. "But there aren't any teachers available so late at night, so the two of us will have private study sessions instead. You should let me know if you have any questions while we're studying."

"In other words, *you're* my tutor." Irina's brow furrowed suspiciously.

"Don't look at me like that," said Lev. "I got pretty good grades, you know."

Really, scheduling study sessions rather than hiring a teacher was Lt. Gen. Viktor's decision. "The test subject doesn't need in-depth knowledge about space travel," he'd said.

Lev decided not to tell Irina that, however, assuming that it would only kill her motivation. When he first saw her, she'd been reading a textbook conscientiously. He wasn't sure what she'd been ordered to learn—if anything—but if she was happy to study on her own, he wasn't about to stop her.

"We're in charge of our meals, the same as our study sessions," Lev continued. "We'll heat pre-prepared food ourselves. There won't be any staff in the cafeteria."

"As long as I have milk, that's fine."

Lev couldn't help smiling at the cold, standoffish vampire's odd preference for such a bland drink. She'd looked utterly adorable wiping milk from the corners of her mouth.

"What're you smiling about?" asked Irina, irritation etched on her face.

"Nothing," said Lev.

"If you think milk's for children, maybe you should swear off it for the rest of your life."

"Huh?"

"If you have a problem with milk, just keep taking shots of zhizni."

Lev thought Irina's reaction to his simple little smile was overly aggressive, but he didn't let that show on his face.

"I'm sorry," he said. "Anyway, let's start training!" As those words left his mouth, he pointed at Irina's tank top and added, "People will think it's strange if you walk around like that in this cold weather. I know it might seem warm, but put your jacket on, all right?"

"I will. Even at twilight, the sun still stings."

At 1700 hours, the evening sun dipped behind the far-off conifer forest, wrapping the world slowly in a blanket of darkness and draping the athletic field in light shadow.

As Lev and Irina stretched and warmed up, Anya arrived in an especially warm-looking scarf.

"Good norning!"

"Er...norning?" asked Lev.

"You know! Because it's nighttime, but you guys just woke up and your day's just starting. *Norning!* What do you think?"

"Uh...it's fine." Lev knew Anya would drag the conversation out if he didn't go along with her.

He called Irina to the four-hundred-meter circuit's starting line. "Running is good for basic endurance," he told her. "We'll run twelve laps total—do them at your own pace."

Irina nodded silently, tapping the ground with her toes. It was hard to imagine a vampire *running*; in legends, they often flew through the night sky. Feeling slightly apprehensive, Lev wondered how well Irina would handle this first training exercise.

Anya hit a button on her stopwatch. "Go!" she cried.

Lev started at a nice, easy pace. He felt it was best for Irina to get used to things slowly; he didn't want to push her too hard.

Irina, however, took off much faster than he expected, running comfortably in front of him. Shrugging, Lev picked up his pace to match. But as soon as he caught up to Irina, she outran him again.

"Wait!" he called. "If you push yourself too hard now, you'll never make it to the end of the night!"

"I'm just running at my own pace," Irina replied. Ignoring Lev's warning, she sprinted ahead.

"You're going too fast!"

"You're just slow!"

As he chased Irina, Lev realized that saying she was "going too fast" might've been a mistake. The girl's running form was beautiful, like a track-and-field athlete's, and she really did seem to be pacing herself.

Irina turned and looked back at him. Her eyes narrowed, and the corners of her mouth crept up. It was the expression of someone who thought they'd already won.

"You asked for it," Lev muttered. "You're a fool if you think you can keep this pace up all night!"

Suddenly feeling competitive, he gave chase. In response, Irina ran faster. Lev couldn't let himself lose to a girl so young. Pursuing her resolutely, he passed Irina.

"You humans! How presumptuous!" Irina called, outrunning Lev again.

"Oh, give me a break!" Lev caught up to Irina immediately and passed her once more.

Both runners breathed raggedly, clearly exhausting themselves. The event had devolved from a morning jog into a battle of personal pride.

"You're going too fast!" Anya called. She couldn't believe her eyes as they ran by her, struggling to pass each other with each lap.

Finally, an exhausted, flailing Lev reached an arm over the finish line.

Anya looked at her stopwatch. Her jaw dropped in shock. "It's...it's a new record."

Between gasps, Lev tried to reply. "Hah, hah... Of course... it is..."

He lay down, stretching across the ground. Cosmonaut candidates competed every day, but he'd never imagined that he'd start Irina's training with a battle of wills against the young vampire. He turned to look at Irina, who sat near the finish line. He was impressed that she hadn't collapsed completely after running full tilt.

Lev sat up and glanced at Anya. "Are vampires' physical abilities better than humans'?"

"No. According to the data, vampires and humans are equally capable on average." In that case, Irina was likely exceptional even among vampires.

Lev and the other cosmonaut candidates had come from military bases across the country, and each had passed harsh tests to make it through the selection process. Lev was in excellent shape and had mental fortitude to match. On the other hand, Mozhaysky had called Irina "an exceptional specimen as capable as the current cosmonaut candidates." Lev's close race with the vampire showed her potential, and he couldn't hide his surprise.

"Did you train for endurance before arriving in LAIKA44?" he asked Irina.

She wiped sweat from her face. "I didn't have a choice," she replied. "The castle I lived in was high on a mountain. I had to climb one thousand, four hundred and eighty steps to reach it."

"That's crazy." One particular detail of Irina's explanation piqued Lev's curiosity. *Huh?* "Sorry, but did you just say 'castle'?"

"Yes. I'm doing you the favor of answering your questions, so would you please do me the favor of listening more carefully, at the very least?"

"But, well...I mean, I'm not used to people casually mentioning *castles*."

It was true that Lev had heard stories about vampires residing in old castles. Was it possible Irina was from a family of nobles? Aristocrats? Lev felt the question on the tip of his tongue, but he stopped it just before it left his mouth. As Lt. Gen. Viktor had said, it wasn't important to know more than necessary about the test subject. Irina's past and family had nothing to do with her training. Besides, the more Lev knew about her, the tougher it'd be for him if the launch failed or Irina was killed in an escape attempt.

Still, Lev wanted to ask. He sighed. It really wasn't easy to close off your heart and become ruthless.

After a short break, Lev and Irina moved to an exam room in the biomedical lab for a complete physical, including x-rays.

Since vampires were Anya's research specialty, she was elated. "Tee hee! This is Irinyan's first detailed checkup since arriving in LAIKA44. I'll *document* her body from top to bottom! Height, measurements, blood pressure, CT scan, EKG, basic metabolic levels... Ha ha ha!"

Her enthusiasm was so overpowering that Irina slowly backed away. "Er..."

"Anya will handle the rest of this," Lev told her. "I'll wait on the other side of this partition." He took a seat, admittedly a little worried about leaving things in Anya's hands. Then he noticed the disdain in Irina's eyes.

"Why're you staying here?" she asked.

"Huh?"

"Are you around when other female candidates have checkups?"

"Uh, no. I'm not."

"Then leave."

"But it's my job to accompany you. And I'll be behind this partition, so it isn't like I'll see anything."

"I don't need your excuses. Your presence bothers me."

"No need to get rid of me completely."

"I said get out!"

"Aha!" Anya raised a finger into the air as though she'd just realized something. "Irinyan...are you embarrassed?"

"I'm no such thing!" Irina's pale skin made it all the more apparent that her cheeks were flushed red.

Lev immediately realized he'd made a horrible mistake. He was suddenly very flustered, his head full of images of Irina unclothed, undergoing her physical. "I-If that's how you feel, you should've told me from the start."

"You're the one who said you'd treat me like any other candidate!"

"Yeah, b-but at the same time, you're a test—"

Irina flashed her fangs as her anger mounted. "You human men are the height of insensitive!"

"All right, all right! I *said* I'm going outside!"

Anya looked back and forth between Lev and Irina with fascination. "Why do you both have bright red ears?"

"Shut up!" Irina snapped.

Lev left the exam room and leaned against a wall, thinking vaguely that Irina's embarrassment was really no different from any ordinary young woman's. He felt ashamed of how rude he'd been because he was too focused on her status as a test subject.

"Yup...I really put my foot in my mouth," he muttered. Staying behind the partition would have only made things awkward.

Lev heard Anya's almost flirtatious voice on the other side of the door, along with Irina's cries.

"Oh, my! Such fair skin! So smooth!"

"Don't gawk!"

"Thin and muscular, but tantalizingly soft!"

"Hey! Don't touch me more than necessary, all right?!"

"Hmm..."

Lev shook his head. "That's Anya for you," he said to himself.

At the same time, he felt curious about what was happening in the exam room. He wasn't comfortable around girls, but he had a healthy interest in their bodies. Clearing his throat, Lev put his ear against the door, listening intently.

"One hundred and fifty-eight centimeters. Forty-three kilograms."

"Wow, she's light." Lev remembered Natalia mentioning that Irina was underweight, but the vampire girl was slighter than he'd expected. "Forty-three kilograms is two twenty-kilo dumbbells," Lev mused, lifting his arms as though gripping imaginary weights in each hand.

"Next, let's take your measurements! Tee hee!"

"Um...why the creepy expression?"

"Bust first! This'll be a little cold, but try not to move, all riiight?"

"Eek! Why're you wiggling your fingers like that?!"

"Hmm...eighty-one or eighty-two centimeters."

Although Lev felt a bit guilty about eavesdropping, he found himself visualizing Irina in her tank top. Under her clothes, was she the same as a human? Pictures flashed through his mind of a dirty magazine someone had smuggled into the dormitory, when—

"Lev?"

Lev leaped in surprise at the voice behind him. "Huh?!"

His heart felt like it had jumped up to his throat. Fighting to put it back in his chest, he slowly turned to see Natalia peering at him.

"Do I need to report you for deviant behavior?" she asked.

"Huh? B-but I'm not doing anything! The door, you see, it's the door! It's so cool and refreshing to touch, and..."

Natalia grinned at Lev's utterly awful attempt at an excuse. "I was just kidding, Lev."

Sweat ran down Lev's back, just as it had when he'd finished running earlier. "But, uh..." He decided the best course of action was to act normal and change the subject. Besides, it was very strange for the dorm matron to be in the biomedical lab. "What're you doing here, Natalia?"

"I heard you'd be here, so I came to let you know how to prepare your meals. Since it's your first day of training, I don't imagine you understand how to warm everything up."

"Ah. Makes sense."

Natalia gave Lev a sheet of paper detailing how to use each of the kitchen's appliances, then left with a wave and a friendly "Good luck!"

Lev sighed in relief.

"St-stop that! It tickles!"

"Aha! You react the same way as a human! How about this?"

"Ah! What kind of checkup is this?! Eek!"

Lev stepped away from the exam room door. He hummed a tune to distract himself and tried to tell himself Irina was just a test subject, even if she happened to be a vampire. Still, her occasional sharp, short cries cut through his defenses.

Irina's physical took about an hour. Afterward, Anya left to summarize the data, and Lev and Irina headed to the dormitory for the night's first meal. For a while, Lev couldn't bring himself to look directly at Irina.

"You're quiet," she said, "and you keep avoiding eye contact. How come?"

"Uh...no reason."

Even under torture, Lev would never admit the things he'd imagined outside the exam room. The thought of Natalia revealing the truth about his eavesdropping was like a knife caressing his neck.

At 2100 hours, the cafeteria was completely empty. Lev and Irina's meals, which had been covered in cheesecloth to deter stray bugs, looked especially lackluster. Their breakfasts consisted of the UZSR's traditional soup, borscht—a broth flavored with pickled beets, carrots, and other root vegetables—and three palm-sized aluminum tubes.

The sight of the tubes twisted Lev's face into a grimace. "Blegh."

"What're these?" asked Irina, picking up a tube. "Toothpaste?"

"Space food."

"What?! Really? I've never seen it before! What's in them?!"

Despite Irina's sudden, mounting excitement, Lev's heart sank. "Well, the National Institute of Medicine's researchers took a scientific approach to blending various foods."

"Wow!" Irina read the text on the tube, eyes alight like a curious child's. Her fascination startled Lev so much that he found himself staring. Irina glared back. "What?"

"I don't know what you're expecting, but it tastes awful. Like baby food. The researchers didn't care about anything except nutrition."

None of the cosmonaut candidates enjoyed space food. Even Lev, who wasn't picky in the slightest, had found himself close to retching the first time he tried it.

Irina ignored Lev's warning completely and pushed a straw into the top of one tube. "Here goes." Her cheeks puckered as she sucked up the space food.

"It's awful, right?"

"It's not that bad."

"Huh?"

"But I *am* disappointed. You called it space food, but it's just normal food." Irina set the tube back on her tray, her interest gone.

"That's anything *but* normal food," Lev muttered.

After seeing Irina's reaction, though, he wondered whether they'd changed the space food's flavor since he'd last tried it. He pushed a straw into one tube and drank. The space food was slimy and watery on his tongue, and its flavor filled his mouth.

"Ugh!" Lev quickly washed the space food down with a gulp of water. Nothing about its taste had changed; it was just as bad as he remembered. "Are your taste buds different from ours or what?" he asked Irina.

"Apparently, you still need teaching." Irina seemed tired of needing to tell him things so often. "Vampires don't have a taste for anything but blood."

"Huh?"

"We can smell food, and we can discern texture and temperature, or intense spiciness. But that chocolate yesterday that the dorm matron said was sweet and delicious? I didn't taste any of that."

"Then what *did* you notice about the chocolate?" asked Lev, a little stunned.

"It was brown, and it had a strong scent and gluey consistency."

Her perplexing answer reminded Lev that, however human she looked, Irina was still a different species.

She offered Lev her aluminum tube of space food. "I don't feel like eating this anymore. I'll give it to you."

"I don't want it! And you have to eat all of it, even if you don't feel like it. Those are the rules."

Irina sighed, spinning the aluminum tube with one finger. Lev understood her disdain for the brand-new food, even though she didn't have a human sense of taste.

"Look, I know you're disappointed," he added. "But the next thing in your schedule is special-equipment training. That'll be tough on both your body and your brain, and it'll only be tougher if you don't get enough energy from your food."

"What kind of special equipment?"

"Stronger versions of the equipment they had you try at the hospital in Sangrad. It involves overheating, spinning... At any rate, it's rough. I'll explain in detail when we get there. For now, just focus on your food."

After warming their borscht up in a pot, Lev and Irina sat across from each other in the cafeteria, which was still empty except for them. Watching Irina sucking up her space food felt surreal to Lev. His parents would be floored if they heard their son was eating space food with a vampire—the very creature he'd been petrified of as a child.

Lev's parents, however, didn't even know he'd been selected as a cosmonaut candidate. The space development program, and by extension the Mechta Project, were classified military operations. Revealing anything about them to the public—including family—was strictly prohibited.

Lev had been recommended for the cosmonaut candidate program nine months earlier. He had been a mere pilot, and he'd just turned twenty-one. He was stationed in a freezing location in the far north, piloting reconnaissance planes.

In early winter, a man from an unknown organization approached him, dressed in black from head to toe. "Would you be interested in flying an entirely new type of supersonic plane at a soon-to-be-established flight school?"

"Just what kind of flying are you talking about?" Lev had asked.

"High-altitude flights around Earth. If you're interested, sit for the exam in Sangrad." The mysterious man listed more details robotically and then vanished like dissipating smoke.

On the surface, the conversation was very suspicious, but Lev's gut told him otherwise.

Hope had filled his heart ever since he'd heard rumors that the UZSR's animal spaceflights would be followed by flights with human passengers. Going to space had been his dream since elementary school; he'd looked up at the night sky and imagined a future flying through the stars. Always believing that his chance would come, he'd worked hard to become an air force pilot.

"High-altitude flights? No way... Rockets?!" Lev had gasped. "I'm going to pass that exam no matter what! Whoo-hoo!" His enthusiasm was a fire that could've melted the tundra itself.

Since Lev was born and raised in a countryside farming region, the exam was the very first time he set foot in the Zirnitran capital, Sangrad. The city's history stretched back to its founding in the twelfth century. With a population of over six million, it was the country's largest city.

Three thousand applicants gathered for the exam at the Military Institute of Medical Science. They were told nothing in detail; instead, they were issued hospital gowns and subjected to roughly ten thorough inspections. Anyone with a single abnormality was summarily sent home, no questions asked. That left a total of two hundred and fifty applicants.

The exam didn't end there. The candidates' careers and family backgrounds were investigated in depth. They completed demanding physical tests that utilized cutting-edge biochemistry. They sat for written tests, during which incorrect answers were constantly announced over loudspeakers. Every method imaginable was used to screen the applicants, until finally only twenty youths remained. Each had intelligence, mental fortitude, and physical abilities of the highest caliber.

At the end of March, when the snow had yet to melt, the air force chief marshal finally revealed the recruitment drive's purpose. "Comrades, rejoice! All of you are cosmonaut candidates, and your goal is space!"

"I...I did it!" Lev could barely hold back the urge to shout. At the same time, he knew he wouldn't be able to share this joy with his family till after his return.

Lev sipped his borscht, thinking about the past, then wondered about Irina's family. Did her parents—who apparently lived in a castle—know their daughter was a test subject? Had Irina herself been kidnapped and forced to take part in the tests? Lev hoped not.

Across from him, Irina brought a spoonful of borscht to her nose and took in its scent—the closest thing she had to the human sense of taste.

Lev wondered whether she'd eaten her roe egg by egg because she wanted to enjoy the texture. *Don't do it, Lev. Don't ask,* he whispered in his heart.

There was too much he desperately wanted to ask Irina. If Mikhail had supervised her, could he have ignored Irina's personhood completely without a second thought? Would he have asked whatever questions he had with cold, clinical distance?

Lev shook his head. *Keep your thoughts on the stars above.* He reached for a tube of space food.

After their silent meal, Lev and Irina stopped by the dormitory toilets before their next training session. Naturally, Lev couldn't follow Irina inside the washroom.

"There're windows in there. You're not going to try to escape, right?" He felt stupid for asking, but he asked all the same.

"I won't run away," Irina replied. "If I try, the death penalty's waiting for me." She went in.

Lev's sigh melted into the darkness of the desolate hallway. "Talk about a tough assignment."

Evening, 2200 hours.

Lev and Irina arrived at the Training Center lobby. They found a smiling Anya awaiting them, binder in hand. "Why, hello there!"

Irina was on guard, perhaps because of what Anya had put her through during her physical; she kept quite some distance from the researcher.

Anya didn't seem to notice. She went over the evening schedule cheerfully. "This session is comprised of load training and a hot room endurance test, right?"

Irina blinked, taken aback. "Hot room...?"

"It's a confined space, like a sauna. We'll assess how long you can endure a high-temperature environment. It gets so hot in there, it's hard to even breathe! Oh, that's right!" Anya exclaimed, remembering. "You're sensitive to heat, aren't you, Irinyan? So the hot room will be especially tough for you." Her voice retained its bright, cheerful tone.

"Why do you...enjoy this so much?" Irina asked.

"Scientists live for experiments! Tee hee!"

The gracelessness of Anya's comment somehow made it even more frightening, and Irina's shoulders slumped.

"I told you it wasn't going to be easy," Lev said as the three walked toward the hot room.

Like the cafeteria employees, most of the Training Center staff had already gone home, leaving behind only night-shift workers and those doing overtime to accommodate Irina's training schedule. It was natural for people working so late at night to be cranky.

However, the vice-director was short-tempered for reasons besides the night shift. "To think *I* have to work with a cursed species. If this weren't a direct order from the chief himself, I assure you, I would've refused outright!" he exclaimed.

Vice-Director Sagalevich was a middle-aged man with white hair. He'd been assigned to observe Irina's special-equipment training. To meet the vampire girl, he'd donned a face mask and gloves, and a cross dangled from his neck. Hatred for Irina emanated from him the moment they met—not unlike the strong garlic stench behind his mask.

"Sending a vampire into space," Sagalevich muttered, making sure to speak loudly enough for everyone to hear. "I can't believe it. We're practically inviting the Lord's rage! We may as well ask Him to send a giant meteor hurtling at us."

"Grr..." Irina bared her fangs.

Lev lowered his voice as he explained, "Vice-Director Sagalevich is deeply religious. He attends church every day."

Lev still remembered what the vice-director had once told him: "The purpose of my work is to prove the existence of God. Go to space and confirm our Lord's existence!" Sagalevich had been deadly serious too. Lev wondered what sort of twisted coincidence had made such a devout believer a vampire's supervisor.

"Whatever you do," Lev told Irina, "*don't* say a word about the church fabricating all those vampire stories, okay?"

He knew they had to tread carefully. Sagalevich had always been ill-tempered and prone to anger. If one of Irina's snide digs at the human race rubbed him the wrong way, he might just erupt.

Irina nodded. "All right. The less I have to talk to another idiot human, the better." She apparently wanted as little to do with the vice-director as possible.

Sagalevich spoke in a low, heavy voice. "In the name of our Lord, let us begin."

The training room was full of data-gathering equipment peppered with flickering red lights. In the center of all the machinery was the hot room. It was about the size of a truck bed. A young engineer named Franz Feltsman was in charge of the equipment. He wore a spotless lab coat that gave off a very clean impression.

"Nice to meet you, Comrade Irina Luminesk," he said.

At Franz's polite greeting, Irina looked at Lev, confused. "This one's so different from that other stupid one."

Lev nodded. "Comrade Franz won't treat you harshly at all. Right, Franz?"

The man leaned in close. "The vice-director and I are completely different," he confirmed in a voice a touch louder than a whisper.

Franz seemed almost *too* conscientious; Lev thought pretty highly of him.

On the other hand, Sagalevich exuded arrogance. He perched on his chair in the corner, clasping his crucifix as though warding off nearby evil. "Franz, enough useless chatter. Let's get this over with."

Franz smiled apologetically. "Who's first?" he asked.

"I'll go first. Irina will go after me," Lev said, taking off his jacket.

He was just about to step into the hot room when the vice-director stood from his chair. "Wait. Who'll watch the vampire while you're in the hot room?"

"Anya and Franz are here. Irina won't run off."

"That's not the issue." Sagalevich slowly pulled a rope and a pair of steel handcuffs from his bag. He threw them toward Lev.

"Huh?!" Lev froze, shocked. He didn't even try to catch the handcuffs, which clattered to his feet with an ominous clang.

"You will bind the test subject," Sagalevich ordered Lev, his gaze cold and hard. "That's a rule."

"But she isn't a dog or—"

"Perhaps *outside*, you have to consider what the common people think. There's no such concern here."

"But Vice-Director..." Lev stood in place, unsure of what to do. Anya put a hand to her mouth, and Franz looked away.

Irina calmly held her hands out. "Put the handcuffs on."

"Huh?"

"If I'm bound, that'll satisfy your human god, right? I can deal with handcuffs and some rope." Although her tone was condescending, Lev was hesitant to bind Irina when she'd done nothing wrong. "Hurry up," Irina added. "I think the old man's afraid I'll bite him."

Her face showed how little she thought of the vice-director, who responded with a glare of his own. The air between them was thick with tension; at this rate, a clash seemed imminent.

"Sorry, Irina," Lev said. He picked up the handcuffs, clamping them over her thin wrists. Then he bound her ankles together and tied the end of the rope to a pillar, looking at the vampire girl with pity.

She gazed back rebelliously. "I hate that look in your eyes."

"But—"

"I *chose* to be tied up. Don't forget that."

"What?" Lev didn't understand what he was hearing; he felt shocked.

She drew her bound hands closer to her chest and stood up straight. "These are just accessories to set him at ease."

Now Lev understood. Irina's dignified posture reflected her rebellious attitude perfectly; her entire body made her feelings clear.

"You may douse me in holy water if you please, O devout and faithful believer," Irina told Sagalevich. She was a step ahead of the vice-director; she'd twisted his ill treatment into something else entirely.

The vice-director's brow furrowed with hatred. He sat back down and again demanded that they start the hot-room training. Irina watched him, letting a snicker escape her nose. Lev didn't know whether she had nerves of steel or she was just stubborn. Still, he was struck by the fact that she was more than a skilled athlete with a pretty face. She also had mental fortitude that might help her through the rest of the cosmonaut training.

"I'll go first so you can see what you're in for," Lev told her. "Hey, Franz, could you give Irina the rundown while I'm in there?"

"Sure."

Body covered in sensors, Lev sat in the hot room for a grueling one-hour period. The temperature reached ninety degrees Celsius; even though he wasn't moving, he broke into a sweat.

"Ugh," he groaned. "It's so hot."

Through a small window in the hot room's wall, Lev watched Franz give Irina a full explanation of the exercise.

"A rocket's cabin holds a cosmonaut. The hot room simulates an emergency situation in the cabin. In some scenarios, the temperature could get extremely high."

Irina listened carefully. "Extremely high...?"

"The cabin's insulated and covered in heat-shield paneling. It should maintain a consistent twenty-degree temperature. But re-entry through Earth's atmosphere causes aerodynamic heating. I'm talking thousands of degrees—it's like wrapping the cabin in flames. In a worst-case scenario, if the cabin wasn't properly prepared, it'd basically be an oven." Franz paused for a moment, breaking eye contact with Irina as his voice grew serious. "In the past, we've lost dogs to the heat."

Irina's lips were pressed straight. She was kneeling, her hands balled into fists.

"One more thing." Franz glanced at Vice-Director Sagalevich. "That guy was the only one who didn't blink when Maly died. He apparently said the dog was just a godforsaken test subject." Franz's eyes darkened. "Maybe one day Sagalevich will receive his own divine judgment."

Lev left the hot room dizzy and unsteady on his feet. "I-I'm dying here."

Franz came over with water and a change of clothes. Gulping the water, Lev finally regained his breath.

"Ahh!" he sighed. "That's the stuff."

Although his body had cried out at the torturous hot-room

training, Lev endured by concentrating on the chance of space travel. Still, he was worried about how much Irina could take, since she'd been brought in as a test subject.

The cosmonauts' special-equipment training wasn't limited to the hot room. It also included artificially induced shocks simulating engine explosions, oxygen deprivation in confined spaces, and pressure training that could burst blood vessels. The training was intended to acclimatize potential cosmonauts to extreme physical and mental distress. But it still wasn't entirely clear what benefit pushing humans to their limits would have for spaceflight. The whole program was being fine-tuned, since space was completely unexplored territory.

Lev untied Irina's feet and took off the handcuffs. "It's really tough in there," he warned her. "And since you're sensitive to high temperatures, it'll just be worse. Say something if it gets to be too much."

"I won't lose to you. I'll sit there for an hour *and* one second."

"No need to be so competitive."

"You just watch me." Irina stormed toward the hot room. The moment she opened the door and felt the heat, however, her face twisted. "This is hell!"

"I told you, didn't I?"

"There's still time to run away." The voice came from Vice-Director Sagalevich. "If you do, though, I can't guarantee your safety."

Sagalevich's eyes narrowed as he watched Irina sit in the hot room, crossing her arms high on her chest.

"I'm ready," she said. "Begin."

As soon as the door shut and the training began, the change in Irina's demeanor was obvious. Her eyes watered, her white skin flushed, and her sweat-drenched hair stuck to her neck and forehead.

Anya raised her voice in concern as she watched through the hot room's window. "She looks like she's going to melt in there."

"Are there any unusual changes in her numbers?"

"They're fine at the moment."

Lev gestured through the window, asking Irina whether she was all right. Irina nodded. Lev couldn't believe how competitive she was. He kept watching, hoping she wouldn't collapse.

Irina made it all the way to one hour and one second.

"W...w-wa...water..." Nearly completely dehydrated, Irina took the water Franz gave her and immediately poured it over her head. "Another glass... Wait. Another five glasses. I need more..."

"Are you all right?" Lev asked.

Irina ran a hand through her hair. "I could do that for another three hours."

"Give me a break."

Still, Lev had to wonder why Irina was so competitive. She'd been the same when they were running. He had a feeling something was motivating her—more than just her dislike of people like Sagalevich, and much deeper than simply not wanting to lose to humans.

"Let's start the next exercise." Sagalevich clapped twice impatiently. He wasn't about to give them a chance to rest. "Hurry up and get ready."

Lev, Irina, and Anya bid a hasty farewell to Franz and moved on to their next training exercise.

Morning, 0030 hours.

They entered the load-training room. The space was about the size of a gymnasium; in the center was a single thick pillar. A long iron frame branched from the top of the pillar, running parallel to the ground. At the bottom of the frame was a box-shaped capsule. The machine was designed to spin a human passenger at high speed, subjecting them to intense load-bearing pressure; it was basically a centrifuge.

Irina stood before the load-training machine, looking at it as though it were an unknown execution device. Her expression was hard, and the sweat on her face still hadn't dried completely. "It's so big... So excessive."

"Compared to the hot room, the centrifuge is easy," Lev said. "It's only five minutes."

"Really?" Irina's expression relaxed.

Lev realized, to his surprise, that the vampire was more expressive than he'd first thought. The hot room had clearly put her through hell, although she'd kept up a tough front.

"So, what kind of training is this machine for?" Irina asked.

"Load training," Lev replied. "Out of all the specialized equipment, the centrifuge is especially important. The hot room prepares you for an unexpected incident, but there's no reaching space without getting past gravity. That's why we do load training."

By definition, a rocket launch pushed against gravity, so cosmonauts would face pressure several times heavier than that on Earth. The force was so extreme that test dogs they'd sent up in the past had been paralyzed, their muzzles bent out of shape and tears streaming from their eyes.

"Er, Lev?" Anya gave him a poke.

"Hm...?" Lev turned to see Vice-Director Sagalevich standing behind him, arms crossed and ready to shout. "We'll begin right away, sir!"

Before the vice-director could make his displeasure clear, Lev got into the centrifuge capsule. He lay in the seat built into the cramped interior, and a supervising engineer secured his body with safety belts. Lev held on to the seat grips; with a heavy rumble, the capsule began rotating.

The human body could withstand twelve times the pressure of Earth's gravity, but the additional load was taxing. It stabbed through a cosmonaut's head and eyes, upset their stomach, and made their blood incredibly heavy. Plus, cosmonauts had to do more than just bear that discomfort—they had to endure it while reading and recording the numbers that flashed on the display panels.

Five minutes later, Lev was released from the hellish capsule. He sighed in relief and exhaustion as he emerged with shaky, trembling legs. "All right, Irina, it's your turn. Don't throw up inside the capsule, all right?"

"Don't underestimate me." Irina shrugged casually, but her expression wavered for a moment—perhaps as fear of the hot room flashed through her mind. Nonetheless, she got into the capsule, and the engineer strapped her in.

Sagalevich's eyebrow twitched as he watched the process. "Strap it in tighter."

"This is entirely sufficient, sir." The engineer looked hesitant but couldn't stand up to Sagalevich; he tightened the safety straps until they dug into Irina's skin.

Lev had a bad feeling, but he couldn't loosen the straps himself. Irina didn't say a word. She and Sagalevich glared heatedly at each other.

"Go ahead," Sagalevich ordered.

The capsule began to spin, and the reading on the centrifuge's monitoring equipment rose slowly from 3 g to 6 g.

Grinning icily, Sagalevich tapped the supervising engineer's shoulder. "The test subject can handle more. Raise the pressure."

The centrifuge groaned as the capsule spun faster. The pressure climbed above 9 g—too much for anyone's first time in the machine.

Lev couldn't take it. He stepped in front of Sagalevich. "Surely that's enough, Vice-Director? It's her first time, and she isn't used to the centrifuge. You'll put too much strain on her."

"Our timeframe to prepare this test subject is extremely limited," Sagalevich retorted. "Are you taking issue with my methods?"

It was as though the vice-director was meting out some kind of punishment to the vampire. Lev was appalled, but the chain of command didn't allow cosmonaut candidates to voice objections to their superiors. Although it was the last thing he wanted to do, he backed down. Since the punching incident, he'd been determined to avoid acts of defiance.

After hitting a full 10 g, the centrifuge finally came to a stop. Irina exited the capsule, extremely pale; after staggering for a moment, she sank to the floor. Lev and Anya rushed over. There were red marks on Irina's white tank top that hadn't been there before.

"What the...?"

Lev looked carefully. His breath caught in his throat as he realized the marks were blood, seeping from where the safety belts had held Irina's body. Friction from the force of the centrifuge's spinning had caused the wounds.

"Are you all right, Irina?"

"It's nothing." Irina gently placed a hand over the blood dirtying her shirt.

"What's the biomed data say, Anya?" asked Lev.

Anya's hand tightened as she checked the readout. "Her numbers are fine, but we need to treat her injuries quickly."

Sagalevich didn't even glance in Irina's direction. Instead, he issued an order to the supervising engineer. "Make sure to wipe the capsule clean with disinfectant and holy water. It's been soiled." It was like he was containing a virus.

The tight straps, and the pain they'd inflicted, had clearly been intentional. Irina glared at Sagalevich and tried to stand, but dizziness seemed to hit her once again, forcing her to stay seated. Lev wanted to say something about the vice-director's hideous behavior, but he could only clench his fists and swallow his rage.

"Well, I believe that's all for today's training." Sagalevich made the sign of the cross and promptly left.

Irina looked utterly dumbfounded. Lev hung his head apologetically. "You'll meet a lot of different people in the space development program. Some of them—like the vice-director—are very narrow-minded. Try not to let them get to you."

"The fact that someone like him rose to a rank like *vice-director* inspires little hope in the human race," Irina spat.

Anya nodded. "When personnel don't look after their test subjects, it's an embarrassment to all us researchers. I'll bring you a first aid kit and change of clothes, Irinyan."

"Perhaps you could disinfect me with holy water while you're at it," Irina replied with a pained smile. Putting her hands on her knees, she slowly rose to her feet.

At least she'd recovered enough to make her usual jabs. Lev felt a little relieved. *Her blood's the same color as mine,* he thought, looking at the red stains on Irina's tank top.

Morning, 0130 hours.

Parting with Anya, Lev and Irina proceeded to their scheduled study time. There was no teacher, no assistants—just the two of them alone. Irina dove straight into reading her textbook conscientiously.

"Like I said, feel free to ask if you have questions," Lev reminded her.

"Please don't talk," replied Irina, not looking up from her book. "You'll break my concentration."

"Oh...sorry."

After studying, they went to the cafeteria for their scheduled meal. Even then, Irina brought her book with her, losing herself in astronomy as she munched her pickled carrots.

Lev always thought of meals as a chance to take a break. Seeing Irina reading so diligently, though, he wondered whether studiousness like hers was necessary if he truly wanted to visit space. He decided he'd also bring a book the next time they ate.

In keeping with her surprisingly focused approach to study, Irina didn't slack off during the strength and endurance training that followed; she did everything expected of her. If Lev had been her instructor, he would've had no choice but to mark her as the top of her class.

Morning, 0300 hours.

Irina sat beside the pool in her bathing suit, taking a short break. The swimming portion of training was over; it'd been a chance for Irina to disprove the myth that vampires were afraid of water.

Lev, sitting next to her, wasn't sure where to direct his eyes. "You tired?"

"I'm fine. Vampires are nocturnal."

Despite Irina's stiff upper lip, she was clearly exhausted. Lev could tell from the quiet of her voice, her bleary expression, and the way she rubbed her thighs.

He stole a glance at her body. Aside from her pointed ears and fangs, there was no telling Irina from any other young woman. If she'd been a seventeen-year-old human, she would've been working or attending high school. Looking at her profile, Lev knew her beauty would've drawn attention either way.

"Hey, Lev." Irina suddenly turned to him. Their eyes met, and Lev quickly turned away. "What is it?" Irina questioned his reaction.

"Hm? Uh, it's just...I was wondering whether your legs hurt," Lev replied.

Irina let out a small sigh and leaned back. "They're fine."

"Anyway, were you going to say something?"

"I was wondering when I'll learn to pilot the spaceship." She tilted her head curiously.

Lev followed suit. "Uh...you won't."

"How will the rocket fly, then? It isn't as though I'll just ride it on autopilot the whole way, is it?"

"They didn't tell you?" Lev was stunned.

"Tell me what?"

Maybe it made sense not to explain how a rocket flew to an animal test subject, but it could cause problems if Irina didn't understand spaceflight. "It's like you just said," Lev replied. "The rocket's fully automated."

"Huh?!" Her jaw dropped.

Lev told her what he'd learned in his lessons. "Arnack's rockets require manual piloting, but Zirnitra's are built with fully automated systems. The chief's rationale is that humans are prone to making mistakes."

"I see," Irina replied. "Well, makes sense. That's pretty much *all* humans do."

The vampire sometimes seemed like a pretty face that constantly spat poison. But since she'd been put in solitary confinement and mistreated, Lev didn't feel he could take issue with that. "Anyway, all you'll have to do is sit in the cabin in the rocket tip and let it take you to space."

Irina nodded, but she seemed a little vexed. "When it comes to technology, I have to hand it to you humans. I don't know exactly how those systems work, but they're amazing."

"I don't understand them in great detail myself," Lev replied. "But apparently, spaceflight is managed by an 8-bit general-purpose mainframe computer with more than five thousand vacuum tubes."

"8-bit, you say..."

"Do you know what that means?"

Irina shook her head. "I don't."

"I knew it."

"But what I *do* know is that those 8-bit computers are smarter than you humans. So your brain's probably *one* bit. My superior brain could have as many as sixteen bits."

Irina tapped the side of her head. Although she'd just admitted that she didn't know how spaceflight technology worked, her face was full of confident arrogance.

To be honest, Lev didn't really care how many bits anyone had. It would've annoyed him to leave things at that, though, so he struck back.

"After launch, the system steers the ship with radio waves," he told Irina. "An artificial brain program makes magnetic tape recordings, handles jettison during the three launch stages to send the rocket through the atmosphere into orbit, adjusts course direction based on instruments that read the sun, and handles atmospheric re-entry to return to Earth."

Irina's eyes widened. "It's all...fully automated?"

"Surely that's all child's play to a superior 16-bit brain," Lev replied. "Right?"

"I-In other words, spaceflight systems are your most stunning technological advancement to date," Irina mumbled. "Sometimes... even you humans can be pretty impressive."

At that moment, there was something adorable about the vampire girl. Lev was tempted to tease her a little more, but he decided that doing so wouldn't be mature. He got to the point. "Anyway, since spaceflight is fully automated, the most important thing for a cosmonaut is preparing their body for launch."

"I see."

"There's one thing that isn't automated—descent by parachute," he added. "That's what we'll do after this. It's a skill every cosmonaut must absolutely master."

"How come?"

"Because there's no way for cosmonauts to land safely inside the cabin."

"Hmm?"

Ideally, Lev explained, cosmonauts would return to Earth inside the cabin with the help of retrorockets. However, that technology still wasn't complete, so the cabin currently didn't decelerate. If someone rode it all the way to Earth, they'd collide with the ground at full speed, ensuring their own death.

"The parachute was devised for pilots in that situation," said Lev.

After the cabin reentered the atmosphere, he continued, the cosmonaut's seat would launch from the cabin at an altitude of about seven thousand meters, and the first parachute would open. That process was automated, but the cosmonaut needed to complete the subsequent steps manually. It was up to them to detach themselves from their seat, open the second parachute, and navigate to a safe landing point. At present, there was no other way to ensure a safe landing.

"Speaking of which, have you parachuted before, or...?"

"Never. I've never even seen someone parachute."

Irina spoke calmly, but it made Lev nervous. It was his job to prepare the inexperienced vampire for a safe solo parachute jump from high altitude within the next two months. Furthermore, the jump would take place *after* Irina returned from space—a feat never before achieved.

When Lev brought up just how difficult this would be, Lt. Gen. Viktor had answered plainly. "As long as the cabin ejects the pilot, there won't be a problem," he'd said. "A trained cosmonaut candidate is capable of opening a parachute and landing safely."

"But isn't there a chance that the gravity load could knock a pilot out at that altitude?" Lev had asked.

"That's why we're using the test subject." In other words, it didn't matter whether the inexperienced Irina's landing failed— even if she broke bones or, in a worst-case scenario, died.

"Something wrong, Lev?"

Lev was startled to suddenly see Irina staring at him. "Uh... no, it's nothing. Just thinking about training."

"Everything will be fine if I can land using a parachute, right?"

"Yeah...uh, exactly."

"Then don't underestimate me. If you can do it, I can too."

Lev didn't understand where Irina's confidence came from. Still, her physical abilities had so far always backed up her words. He just had to believe she was right.

Fortunately, they wouldn't be practicing the fast-paced parachute descent required for special forces troops landing in battle zones. Cosmonauts landed more slowly. As long as Irina didn't pass out upon re-entry, chances were she'd land safely.

"Well, let's get changed and get out there," Lev said.

Dense fog clouded the deep-blue sky that had yet to dawn. Lev and Irina had reached the parachute training facility located outside of town.

The facility consisted of two structures. The first was an eighty-meter steel-frame descent tower for practical parachute training.

That installation doubled as a watchtower; a searchlight at its peak lit the grounds below. The other was a twenty-two-meter parachute tower designed to accustom candidates to the fear of heights. The top of the structure was designed to look like the body of an aircraft. Jumpers harnessed themselves to wires so they could leap from the door, practice their descent, and be safely carried to a landing point without opening an actual parachute.

"We'll start at the parachute tower," Lev said.

"Looks fun."

"Compared to everything else we've done, yeah, it really is fun. The view from your parachute—high up in the sky, looking down—is seriously amazing!"

After reaching the top floor and putting on her helmet, Irina stood at the dive point and donned her harness.

Lev taught her the basic fall posture. "Cross your arms, lower your head, and push your jaw into your chest. If you don't keep your jaw tucked, you'll end up with whiplash."

Irina didn't move. She was frozen in place.

"What's wrong?" Realizing that something was off, Lev leaned in to check on her. The vampire girl was rigid, as though she'd seen something terrifying. Her body trembled, and her breathing was ragged. "Irina?"

She didn't respond.

No way, Lev thought. *It can't be.* "Are you scared?"

"N-n-no! I m-mean—no, I'm not!" She was clearly rattled; her face was pale.

"Your forehead's sweating."

"Y-y-you're j-just imagining things!" Wiping the sweat from her brow, Irina tried to back away from the door. The harness pulled against her, trapping her in place. "Augh!"

"Hey, now..." Lev said, trying to calm her down.

Irina turned to him, teary-eyed. "A-anyway..."

"Hm?"

"Can't we wait till the retrorocket technology is ready?"

The sudden left turn caught Lev off guard. "The people at the top concluded that, if we wait, the UK will beat us to it."

"You humans and your utterly stupid need to compete!" Irina spat the complaint, sounding irritated, but her legs quivered.

"Your knees are knocking," Lev pointed out.

"Th-that's because this is so exciting!" She tried to speak with conviction, but at the same time, she was tightly gripping the rails on either side of her.

"Come on, now."

There was absolutely no mistaking it: Irina was afraid of heights. Realizing that, a question flashed through Lev's mind—what about all those stories about vampires flying through the night skies? And why had Irina been brought in as a test subject? It was silly to try to make someone with a fear of heights a cosmonaut.

Then Lev realized that nothing in the tests and inspections he'd taken to enter the cosmonaut candidate program had checked whether he was afraid of heights. Of course they hadn't; the applicants were pilots pulled from across the UZSR. It was inconceivable that any of them would feel uncomfortable at high altitudes.

Lev asked Irina about the tests to make sure.

"No, th-they didn't t-test me at high altitudes," she said.

Just as he'd thought, the officials had probably believed the old rumors and myths about vampires flying too.

"Have you ever been on a plane?" Lev asked.

"Never. When they brought me here and to the capital, it was by truck."

The thought of Irina being dragged back and forth filled Lev with pity. At the same time, however, he had to imagine what'd happen if he reported Irina's acrophobia to Lt. Gen. Viktor. If she couldn't jump from a cabin, she'd be written off. Given what she'd now seen and learned, she'd end up in the mines or perhaps even dead. And, of course, Lev's inability to fulfill his duties would be its own problem.

In light of that, Irina had to overcome her fear for both of their sakes. As Lev stood before the cowering Irina, he decided to do whatever it took, even if that meant becoming a monster.

"At the Air Force Academy," he told her, "scaredy-cats went through a trial by fire."

"Lev? Wh-what's with that scary look on your face? Lev...?" Irina's voice was so quiet, it almost vanished entirely. Lev took hold of her collar. "Eek! Wh-what are you doing?!"

He dragged the struggling Irina to the dive door and held her upright at the entrance. "Chin to chest!" he shouted. "Otherwise, you'll get whiplash!"

"W-wait! Wai—"

Lev pushed Irina out the dive door. "Fly!" he said, uttering a million apologies in his heart.

"Ah!" Irina was so frightened, she barely managed a scream. Her body plummeted, hanging from her harness. "Eep..." She slid down the wire, her body stock-still.

Lev went to meet Irina at the landing zone. He found her still in her harness, her form limp like a lifeless, broken puppet. "You alive in there?"

For a while, Irina didn't even try to get up.

"What's wrong?" Lev asked again. "Did you get hurt?"

The vampire fidgeted hesitantly, embarrassed. "Give me a hand," she mumbled. "I can't get to my feet."

"You really were terrified, huh?"

"Because you pushed me!" The tears in Irina's eyes weakened her glare. "You should be ashamed."

"Okay, okay." Lev unclipped the harness and pulled Irina to her feet. He was surprised by how light she was. He'd imagined her weight as similar to a heavy set of dumbbells, but actually picking her up was more like lifting a child. "There we go."

"Hey, Lev."

"Hm?"

"If you tell anyone about this, I'll bite you." Standing upright, Irina stared at Lev with utter humiliation written on her face.

"I won't say anything," he replied. "Don't worry. I don't really want to get bitten either."

Since meeting Irina in her cell, Lev had thought of her as an ice-cold vampire princess. Yet now, sharing this secret, he felt— for the first time—a kind of closeness; a connection.

✦ ◆ ✦

As the eastern skies lightened, Lev and Irina left the training towers. They headed to the dormitory for another meal.

"Now for the last item on the schedule," Lev told her. "This is how training will go for the next two months."

"Too easy," Irina replied, putting her earlier fear of heights out of mind.

"Let's have a drink before we head off. I'm thirsty. Besides, it's kind of a post-training tradition." Lev led Irina to a roadside vending machine for soda water.

"What's this?" she asked.

"You haven't seen one? Let me show you how it works."

Lev washed out the glass cup beside the machine, then placed it in the vending machine and inserted a copper coin. When the machine filled the cup with soda water, he took it and gulped the water down, one hand on his hip.

"Ah! That's the stuff. Want to try some, Irina?"

Irina had been watching Lev very intently. She blinked a few times. "How is soda water different from regular water?"

"You've never had it?" Soda water was common all over the UZSR, but it made sense that there weren't vending machines deep in the Lilitto mountains. "You've got to try it. It's refreshing and delicious!"

"You know I can't taste anything," Irina said with a pout.

"Don't worry—it's not the taste so much as the effervescence that makes it good. I'll buy you a cup." Lev refilled the glass with soda water and passed it to Irina.

She brought it to her nose and sniffed carefully. "Hm...? Something's popping in the water. What is this liquid?"

Lev felt his playful, prankster side emerging. "Scared of a little soda water? You know, some humans drink it in a single gulp."

The words needled Irina; she turned to Lev with a sharp glare. "Who said I was scared? I, too, can drink this in a single gulp!" She brought the glass to her lips, tilted it, and drank the soda water with great gusto. "Hm?!" Her eyes widened. "Wha—?! Wah...ah..."

Irina stuck out her tongue, and the cup dropped from her hand as if she'd just drunk poison. She squirmed, rubbing her throat as it itched with a new sensation. Lev laughed so hard he had to hold his stomach.

"You tricked me!" Irina's white cheeks flushed red with embarrassment.

"I-I'm sorry! It's just... Ha ha ha!"

"Stop laughing! I'll never touch a human beverage again!"

Lev bent to pick up the cup, flashing a smile at Irina. "But it was good, wasn't it? Refreshing, right?"

"Refreshing? Hm..." Irina cocked her head and put a finger to her lips. Her eyes widened again. "Not in the slightest!"

"You had to think about it, didn't you?"

"Shut your mouth! I'm going to bite you!" She bared her fangs.

Lev kept smiling as he washed the cup; he'd enjoyed the prank. "Lemon seltzer's definitely the best, though," he added.

"L-Lemon seltzer?"

"Soda water and lemonade. It smells like lemons, and it's even more refreshing than ordinary soda water."

"Hmm." Something about that clearly piqued Irina's interest, but she suddenly stopped herself, asking, "So what?"

"If you want to try lemon seltzer sometime, I'll get you some."

"I said I don't want human beverages!"

"I think you'd like the scent, though. And you have to admit, soda water is good, right?"

"I hate it! It was more nauseating than holy water!" Apparently if something was man-made, Irina didn't want to like it, no matter what it was.

"You don't need to put on that song and dance, you know."

"All you have to get me is milk. Milk, you hear me?!" Enraged, Irina began to storm off.

"Hey!" Lev called. "That's not the way to the cafeteria."

"I knew that!" She turned on her heel and rushed past Lev, covering her cheeks in an unsuccessful attempt to hide her flushed ears and forehead.

Lev had to hold back the urge to laugh. *Just how stubborn can this girl be?*

Morning, 0900 hours.

Their last meal over, Lev and Irina returned to the cells to shower. Irina grabbed the change of clothes awaiting her in the guard room.

"No peeking," she said before entering the shower room.

Lev sat by the door, mind drifting. "Ahh... What a day." He'd felt so tense supervising Irina that he was more exhausted mentally than physically. "But, man, the way she looked when she drank that soda water!" He chuckled.

In retrospect, it seemed so silly that he'd hid his neck when he met Irina. The beautiful, self-possessed vampire despised humanity; she wasn't officially classified as human, and she had unique abilities that set her apart. When Lev was with Irina, though, he constantly fell for the illusion that she was just another young human woman.

"But she's really a test subject." That fact slipped away from him whenever he wasn't focused on it.

Lev found himself thinking about Irina's silhouette praying at the monument for dogs lost to the space program. As she'd looked at the sky at that moment, what went through her mind? She was always so strong-willed and calm, but was she really prepared to potentially sacrifice her life?

"Damn it. I just can't do it," Lev said to himself. "I can't treat her as an object."

The more he thought about Irina, the more wrapped up in the situation his emotions got. He couldn't stop them. He thought back to the order he'd received: "Complete all required training and examinations without failure until the test launch."

Something stirred deep in Lev's chest. He was responsible for the period before the launch, but the success of the launch itself was out of his control. Whether Irina ended up as a monument, like Maly had, was in God's hands.

Lev sighed. He'd been prepared to carry a burden of sorrow on this journey, but it'd grown very heavy, very quickly. Still, as he listened to the running shower, he felt that he and Irina could still make it.

"Whatever happens at the launch happens," he murmured. "For now, we need to do something about her fear of heights."

SCARLET EYES
• ОЧИ алый •

Water ran over Irina's head and face. To her, the shower was lukewarm, but it would've felt cold to any human. Her lustrous black hair flowed down her back to her hips as if blanketing her. Her thin, fragile-looking collarbone had bruises from the centrifuge straps. It was puffy, and it ached.

Letting out a long, heavy sigh, Irina thought back to the parachute tower. "He saw my weakness."

The moment she'd looked down at the ground, her body had quivered, and her legs refused to move. She had imagined falling through the sky and suddenly felt sick, heart pounding in her chest. Irina never thought she'd balk during her training, and she despised herself for it.

"Will it get easier the more I do it?" she thought aloud.

Running the soap over her body, she decided to think about something else. The first thing that sprang to mind was soda water. The moment she'd drunk the beverage, she'd felt like her mouth was going to melt or explode. But the soda water had also been fizzy and refreshing. It cleared her head and refreshed her with the kind of shock she hadn't felt since she first drank goat's blood.

"I wonder what lemon seltzer tastes like?"

Her hands froze in place for a moment as she lost herself thinking of the mysterious lemon-scented beverage.

"No!" she said suddenly, coming to her senses. "I won't tolerate a human beverage."

Irina shook her head. Cow's milk was enough for her. After all, to the humans, she was nothing more than an object to use to achieve their dreams. For now, she'd let them use her.

Even after she'd washed the dirt from her body, though, she couldn't wash away the darkness rooted in her heart.

CHAPTER 3

Night Flight

INDIGO EYES
• ОЧИ ИНДИГО •

LEV HAD BEGUN supervising Irina's training two weeks ago. Sundays were days off, but Irina said she had books to read, and she showed no desire to leave her cell. Since he finally had a little time to himself, Lev headed to his regular haunt, Jazz Bar Zvezda.

Jazz Bar Zvezda was a hole-in-the-wall full of wafting cigarette smoke, with only eight seats around a single table. Lev sat at the far end of the counter, letting his body sway to the pleasant jazz playing on the bar's electric phonograph. He ordered a shot of chilled nastoyka and drank it in a single gulp. Its stiff kick warmed his core, and he let out a satisfied sigh.

Lev had passed a few cosmonaut candidates en route to Zvezda, but they'd done little more than exchange greetings; not a word was asked or spoken about Irina. Lt. Gen. Viktor had already told everyone that they didn't need to know more than necessary about the vampire. The candidates were following his orders so diligently that Lev felt they were keeping him at arm's length.

"I wonder if Irina's still hitting the books in her cell?" Lev had come to Zvezda to clear his head, but before he knew it, his thoughts were once again on the vampire girl.

Vice-Director Sagalevich's abusive training had continued, but through it, Irina had learned to handle extreme conditions quickly. She'd improved to the extent that, after each exercise, Sagalevich was left seething as he clutched his crucifix. Her checkups and other training sessions were also going smoothly; the only issue was her parachute training.

Lev had hoped that Irina would get used to heights after a while. However many times she ziplined from the parachute tower, though, her trembling never ceased. When Lev had resorted to "shock therapy," sending Irina off the taller descent tower with her parachute open, she'd almost fainted. On top of that, she'd labeled him an "attempted vampire killer." At this rate, there was no way she'd make a successful landing. She'd almost certainly pass out at the seven-thousand-meter descent point.

"We have to find *some* way to overcome that," Lev muttered.

He couldn't sit still, so he left Jazz Bar Zvezda with no real destination in mind.

Before a scheduled study session, Lev suggested, "I'd like to do special training today to help overcome your fear of heights."

Even Irina had admitted to her fear by now, so she didn't argue that particular point. "What kind of training?"

"Well, I went to the library and did a lot of research, but, uh... I only found human strategies for overcoming a fear of heights," Lev admitted.

"Human strategies?" Irina pouted in displeasure.

"Look, just hear me out, all right?"

"Fine."

Lev opened his notepad and read the contents. "First of all, telling yourself that heights aren't scary only works against you. You're scared of heights because you'll die if you fall. That reaction's innate, like an animal instinct, so you shouldn't just try to ignore it."

"Hmm."

"They also say that a powerful imagination is one reason for this kind of fear. Have you pictured what might happen if you hit the ground from high up?"

"I have," Irina said.

"You need to wipe those scary images away and replace them with more positive ones. For instance... Your castle's up in the mountains, right? You could concentrate on how it's really beautiful up that high, looking down at the scenery."

"How about looking down at *humans*?" Irina's voice was as casual as her expression was cold.

The venomous comeback set Lev off balance; he cringed for a second. "Er...anything else you could look at?"

"Hmm. Well, when I'm parachuting, the stars will be...closer."

"Yes! Yes! They're beautiful from up high," Lev agreed and

then checked his notebook. "Some people also get used to heights by standing on a roof for ten minutes at a time. You'll be jumping from seven thousand meters, though—that's way beyond the height of everyday buildings."

"In that case, what other options are there?"

"We're going to change up our schedule so we can try something...a little drastic," Lev replied.

"D-drastic...?"

Lev flashed his ID—which let him access the military airfield—at the trembling Irina. "We'll take a two-seat trainer plane through the skies," he replied.

"We're going flying?!" Irina was so shocked, she almost fell over.

"It feels amazing up there!" Lev insisted. "Your fear will blow away on the wind."

"A-and...you'll be the pilot?"

"Of course! It *has* been ten months since I last flew, though." Lev gave Irina a thumbs-up, flashing a grin.

Irina still seemed shocked, but Lev couldn't stop telling her how good it felt up in the sky, simultaneously assuring her that they absolutely wouldn't crash. Irina finally agreed, trying to convince herself that she really would be fine.

At 0400, Lev and Irina arrived at the military airfield some ten kilometers from LAIKA44. They sat in the trainer's cockpit as it sped down the runway, which was lit by guidance lights.

Lev sat in the pilot's seat, in front of Irina. "You don't have anything to worry about!" he told her through the radio in the oxygen mask he wore.

"A-all right!"

Glancing at Irina in the rearview mirror, Lev saw that she'd shrunk in on herself. Both her hands gripped her jacket sleeves, her eyes shut tightly.

He checked the trainer's speed. "V1..."

The plane's seats reverberated as its engines blasted and its wheels rolled roughly over the ground. Guidance lights sped by in the distance.

"VR..." Lev continued. "And...takeoff!"

The trainer now at full throttle, Lev pulled the control yoke toward himself. The plane lifted off the ground, gently rising into the air.

"Eek!" Irina let out a short cry, then asked, "Are we...are we flying?"

"Uh-huh. And it's only up from here!" A night sky of twinkling stars spread above the cockpit canopy, and the marshland swamps below reflected the moon. "What do you think? It's pretty, isn't it?"

"It's all black," Irina muttered, her eyes shut tight. Shivers ran through her body.

"Then open your eyes!"

"All right, fine." Her eyes opened a fraction, her head moving erratically, like a squirrel searching for danger.

"Look up and right," Lev told her.

Shifting her gaze nervously to where he said, Irina gasped. The moon floated in the sky before her, shining a beautiful silver. "Oh!"

Just moments ago, she'd been so terrified. Now, however, she was completely taken with the scenery. It was like the moon itself had cast a spell to conquer her fears. Irina stared in silence.

"Are you still scared?" Lev asked.

She put a hand to her chest, letting out a breath. "I don't know anymore. My heart's racing."

"You look pretty comfortable to me."

"Do I?"

"Well, you aren't trembling anymore. And your eyes are wide open, aren't they?"

"Huh?" Lev's words surprised Irina.

A bright smile grew on Lev's face, as if the change in Irina had changed him as well. "The first time I flew on my own," he said, "it was like I'd grown a pair of wings. Freed from the ground below, basically my whole perspective on life changed. That's why I hope it isn't fear you feel at this point, but freedom."

"Freedom..." To Lev's eyes, Irina looked to be on the verge of understanding.

He decided to keep flying. "We'll be breaking from my plan a little, but let's go to the next level. We'll climb to seven thousand meters and do some load training!"

"What? W-wait! Who said anything about that?!" Irina cowered in her seat as it vibrated.

Lev didn't relent. "There's nowhere to run to, so hang on tight!" He pulled the yoke, raising the trainer's nose. "Don't even think about shutting your eyes this time. Engaging the afterburner!"

Brilliant red flames shot from the exhaust as the trainer picked up tremendous speed. The pressure pulled the skin on Irina's face tight. "Eeeeek!"

They burst through the wandering clouds, climbing to higher and higher altitudes. In less than a minute, the trainer plane entered a sea of stars, with nothing above to block the view. As the trainer gently resumed horizontal flight, Lev and Irina's bodies grew light. It was this moment and sensation—when the body and the mind both felt released—that Lev loved.

"We're here!" he said.

Irina wheezed. "You were...trying to kill me... I know it!"

Lev felt her resentful gaze against his back as he pointed to the endless sky stretching above them. "When you're released from the cockpit after coming back from space, you'll be up this high."

Heart now calm, Irina stared at the sparkling stars above with deep admiration. "It's hard to even imagine."

"We'll fly around a bit so you can get used to this altitude."

"All right."

This training flight for Irina was the first time Lev had climbed into a cockpit in a while. Flying through the borderline zone between the ground and space uplifted his very soul. Did zero gravity feel completely different from high-altitude flight? Lev imagined the sight of Earth from space—that beautiful sphere of blue. It was true that some scholars believed that seeing Earth in such an impersonal way would cause a cosmonaut a mental breakdown, but he was sure he could bear it.

He'd never realize his dreams of that experience as a cosmonaut candidate reserve, though. The only one who would was the young vampire girl who sat quietly behind him, awed by the scenery above.

"Hey, Irina," Lev called, still gazing ahead.

"What?"

"Nothing. Never mind." His sentimental thoughts and feelings about space had been on the tip of his tongue. He'd never vented to anyone, but for some reason, he wanted to open up to Irina. "If you start feeling sick, let me know," he said instead.

Although Lev was looking after Irina, he also felt a little jealous that she'd go to space soon. He knew that, if he were ordered to act as a test subject for a flight, he would've jumped at the opportunity. At the same time, he realized that part of him wanted this girl with her hatred of humans to succeed. Not because that was his job or duty—simply because he wanted to see her efforts rewarded.

As dawn neared, the world turned a deep navy color. At the same time, the steep mountain ranges hidden in the darkness slowly revealed themselves in the far northwest. Those mountains separated the UZSR and Lilitto. They'd seen constant battle in the time of the Great War, but the beautiful, snowcapped mountains showed no trace of that dark history from this high above.

"Your hometown's over there, right?"

"Mm..." Irina stared out the window. Her gaze was wrapped in a sorrow she'd never let Lev see before.

"Shall we get a little closer?" he asked.

His question seemed to bring her back to reality. As she realized she'd revealed a part of herself she wanted hidden, her usual expression returned.

"No," she replied, her tone a mix of loneliness and anger. "Go back down. The sun's rising."

Although Lev wondered what had happened in Irina's hometown before she left, she was right about the sun. He had to consider the trainer's fuel level too. He pushed the yoke forward. Irina kept silent throughout the plane's descent; Lev felt awkward and unsure of what to say.

It wasn't until they were closer to the ground that she spoke through the radio.

"Thank you."

"Huh?" At first, Lev thought he'd heard wrong—those weren't words he was used to hearing from Irina. He peered at her in the rearview mirror.

She stared past the plane's canopy and spoke again. "Thanks to you, I think I can get used to this."

"Oh. Well, that's great." Lev couldn't make out Irina's exact expression—it was hidden behind her oxygen mask—but he sensed that she felt somewhat bashful.

That is, until she met his gaze and kicked the back of his seat sharply, shouting, "Look where you're going!"

Her voice pierced his eardrums, almost making him yank the control yoke. "Please don't yell like that," Lev replied, turning back toward the front of the trainer.

Still, after observing a little gratitude from the ever-standoffish Irina, Lev felt they'd come to understand each other in some small way. He gazed at the horizon, which was slowly turning pale white.

I knew it, he thought. *There's freedom in the skies.*

When they returned to the airfield, everyone was rushing around for some reason. It wasn't yet dawn, but transport planes were being prepared for launch.

"What the...?" Lev murmured.

He and Irina looked on, confused, as a loud trolley passed by quickly. On the trolley was a box labeled "for emergency blood transfusions." There was no doubt now that something had happened somewhere.

"What's going on?" Lev asked a man nearby.

The man glared until Lev flashed his ID. Then he answered curtly, "There was an accident at Albinar. Several technicians sustained injuries."

Something about the answer didn't sit right with Lev, but he had no luck getting more information, and the man soon left.

"Albinar?" Irina repeated.

She looked confused, so Lev told her something no regular citizen was aware of. "That's where rockets and artificial satellites launch from."

The Albinar Cosmodrome was another closed administrative-territorial formation. The city had been built in a remote rocky desert near the equator, two thousand kilometers southeast of LAIKA44.

"But if the accident involved technicians, why are they sending blood from so far away?" Irina asked.

Failure was to be hidden; that was how the Zirnitra Union worked. Lev felt unsettled. He was sure there was more to the accident that he hadn't been told.

In the end, Lev's hunch proved correct. The national broadcast said that the state commission chairman had passed away suddenly in a plane crash, but that was merely a way to hide the truth from UZSR citizens.

It wasn't until two days after the accident that Lt. Gen. Viktor revealed the shocking truth. An explosion during an intercontinental ballistic missile test had caused a hundred and fifty deaths, including that of the chairman of the state commission. The explosion was ascribed to "faulty electric circuits and numerous technician errors," but there were also worrying rumors that somebody—or some group—had conspired to sabotage the test.

The threat wasn't likely to be spies from the UK, but rather, saboteurs from within the Zirnitra Union itself.

Although the UZSR had over twenty space programs—including a program for planetary exploration—the national budget was limited, so those helming each program typically did anything and everything to safeguard their budgets. Although Korovin had a thousand people working for him, he required the National Institute of Science's support. Powerful heads of state also backed scientists in the camp of his political rival, Graudyn. Since Lev's dream was simply to reach space, it depressed him to learn the truth—that the world was drowning in greed and ambition.

"There's no way I can tell Irina what's going on behind the scenes," Lev mumbled. She already had a strong distrust of humans, and he didn't want it to grow any worse.

The tragedy at Albinar negatively impacted even the Mechta Project. Since the dead chairman had held managerial power within the project, rocket development paused until a replacement could be confirmed. That, in turn, caused the suspension of cosmonaut candidate training, including Lev and Irina's.

Higher-ups placed restrictions on the use of the special training facilities and aircraft, so Lev and Irina focused on drills at the parachute tower. Their routine consisted of leaping from the eighty-meter descent tower onto a mat on the ground while wearing an open parachute. That exercise was generally used to practice five-point landings and correct landing posture, but in Irina's case, it was primarily meant to help her overcome her fear of heights.

"Eek!" Irina cried from above, gently hanging from her open parachute.

Lev shouted advice from the ground. "Don't forget how to do your five-point landing! The balls of your feet, then the side of your calf, the side of your thighs, hip, then back!"

"I-I know!" Irina's landing was awkward and stiff; her extra momentum made her fall flat on her face. "Ow!"

Her jumps were smoother now than when she'd trembled the whole way and landed on her butt. As far as Lev was concerned, the fact that Irina could leap from the tower at all was a huge step forward. Still, she wasn't improving as quickly as they'd hoped, and parachuting from a plane was something else entirely.

Irina stood up, her eyes watering. The tip of her nose was bright red. "I hit my nose."

"Let's, uh...let's take a break, all right?"

The pair sat on the landing mat's edge, chatting as they drank from their water bottles. The night wind was chilly, and Lev had closed his jacket tightly, but Irina showed no sign of discomfort.

"By the way," she said, "What's happening with that accident in Albinar? Is it possible they'll cancel the project?"

The question made Lev nervous, but he didn't let it show. If the Mechta Project were canceled, Irina's test flight would be put on hold indefinitely; however, the top brass were acting as though the project was still going ahead. He didn't want to talk about it in depth. All the same, he didn't intend to lie to Irina, so he decided to gloss over it. "It seems like it'll continue. They'll pick a new chairman in the next few days."

"I see." Irina's voice was little more than a mutter, and it was difficult for Lev to read her feelings. He scrambled for something else to say, but Irina spoke first. "I've been wondering. Why did that missile explode at the cosmodrome?"

"Engine fuel."

"No, I mean, why test a missile there?"

"Wait," Lev said. "Do you know why the UZSR wants to use rockets in the first place?"

Irina looked confused. "To go to space, right?"

"No. To use as tactical weapons."

"What do you mean?" Her face suddenly darkened.

"Instead of firing a nuclear warhead at the UK, we're sending cosmonauts to space in rockets because cosmonauts are human missiles! We might even scare God into running away!"

That was a popular joke among the cosmonauts, but Irina didn't seem to find it even remotely funny.

"I'm kidding," Lev added. "I really hope the UZSR's just developing rockets to travel into space."

Irina stared into his eyes. "Will we really see that kind of future? A future where rockets are only developed for space travel?"

"Well, that's a bit of an idealistic prediction." Lev scratched the back of his head, grinning wryly.

"Do you mean that not many humans think like that, the way you do?"

The question was honest, naive, and a bit childlike. Lev felt awkward as he struggled to answer. "Most people working on the ground—the cosmonaut candidates, engineers, technicians—hope rockets aren't used for war. The Space Race doesn't matter to us; we're only chasing our dreams. It's just that we can't really stand up and say that out loud."

"Why not?"

"We'd be taken off the project."

The corner of Irina's lips twisted downward. "That's ridiculous."

"It's better than it used to be," Lev replied. "It was much worse during the war. The secret police took my old teacher."

"Took...?"

Lev stared at the crescent moon fading in the distance. "It was right before the war ended. My teacher told us 'Aircraft are meant to fly the skies—they aren't weapons of murder.' The very next day, that teacher vanished from the village. Speaking the truth is all it takes to become an 'enemy of the people.'"

"That's horrible," Irina whispered, staring at Lev's face.

Lev nodded gently. He put a hand to his chest. "If my teacher's still alive out there somewhere, I hope they get a chance to see me become a cosmonaut."

"I hope they're safe."

Lev looked at Irina. Her eyes were downcast. He shut his mouth; he'd said too much. Although the war was over, his comments could land him in trouble if the Delivery Crew overheard them. So why had he even brought this up with Irina?

"Well, that's all the time we have for history. Let's get back to training." Lev put away his water bottle as a sign that the conversation was over.

A week after the Albinar accident, the chairman's replacement was appointed. First Secretary Gergiev ordered the Mechta Project to resume, and the special training facilities and airfields reopened for use.

"That entire accident occurred because we're insisting on sending a cursed species to space!" declared the ever-incendiary Vice-Director Sagalevich.

Irina ignored him, and her special training proceeded smoothly. The vampire had reached the point where she could do a successful five-point landing from the parachute tower, so she was finally ready for high-altitude parachute training. Naturally, she wouldn't be left to her own devices her first time. She'd start off with a tandem jump, which meant her supervisor, Lev, would be strapped behind her.

Morning, 0300 hours.

Powdered snow danced in the freezing dead of night. A helicopter, its pilot assigned by Lt. Gen. Viktor, flew Lev and Irina up into the sky. When they reached maximum altitude, high enough to look down at the clouds, they got ready to jump.

Both Lev and Irina wore helmets and flight jackets to stave off the cold, and Irina's back was harnessed to Lev's midsection. They sat at the helicopter's open door; Irina was frozen solid.

Lev leaned close to her ear, talking her through the descent. "When you get back from space and the cabin ejects, you'll open your parachute like you're sitting on a swing. It's a little different from a regular descent. But it never hurts to cover the basics." Irina remained silent, as if Lev's words went in one ear and out the other. Lev knocked on her helmet. "Hey."

Irina snapped back to attention. "Wh-why're we jumping from here? I-Isn't it t-too high?"

"I'll handle everything this time around," Lev continued. "You can just leave it all to me."

"B-but..."

"It'll be a little cold. There's no wind, though, so it should be a nice, easy jump. But no kicking or struggling, okay? If we get tangled in the parachute cords, we'll plummet to our deaths."

Irina bared her fangs. She seemed to be on the verge of tears. "Is that a threat?"

Lev laughed. "All right, let's get in position to exit. Cross your arms over your chest and grab your shoulders."

Irina's fingers gripped her jacket so tightly she almost ripped it. She took a deep breath to prepare herself.

"All right," Lev said. "Three! Two! One! Zero!"

At the end of his quick countdown, he jumped from the helicopter without hesitation. He helped the frozen Irina outstretch her arms and legs, then let out the drogue parachute.

"We aren't stopping! Why not?!" Irina shrieked after the drogue parachute was deployed. "Didn't you open the parachute?!"

"Don't worry! That wasn't the main parachute. The drogue parachute is to stabilize us and slow us down."

"Then open the *main* parachute already!"

"Calm down! This is less like falling than riding a pillow through the sky, don't you think?"

"Er...ah...um...!" Irina was in a complete panic. Lev couldn't see her, but it was all too easy to imagine her strained expression.

"We're still in freefall!" he yelled. "Make sure you keep stretching your arms and legs wide!"

"L-Like this?!" Irina extended her limbs tentatively.

"That's it! Now lift your head and arch your back!"

With Lev's guidance, Irina managed the right posture. Before long, however, she began flailing in discomfort. "Ugh! I can't... breathe!"

"Cover your nose with both hands! That'll lower the wind resistance and make things a little easier!"

Irina did as Lev suggested and sighed in relief. She'd been a nervous wreck initially, but as time passed, she settled down and their fall stabilized. They passed through the clouds, free falling as powder snow danced around them in the sky.

"This is fantastic!" Lev shouted.

"The ground's closing in! Why aren't you using the main parachute?!"

"Hey, easy now! I'm deploying it!"

The main parachute filled with air and opened wide, slowing their descent to a gentle sink. Irina heaved a great sigh of relief.

"So, how was it?" asked Lev.

"Chills are still running through my body."

"There's a lot we need to work on to ensure you return safely from space," Lev reminded her. "The landing itself, water landings, strong winds, spin recovery, measuring the distance to the ground. We'll get your body used to it all bit by bit."

"Understood..."

A few minutes later, they touched down. Irina immediately collapsed onto the ground.

Lev unclipped the harness. "Are you all right? Do you think you can stand?"

Irina stumbled forward as she stood up on her own. Brushing the grass from her jacket, she stood tall, her resolve clear in her expression. "Do we have time for one more jump today?"

"Huh?" Lev's eyes widened at Irina's completely unexpected question.

"We've still got time before dawn, right? I want to practice everything again before I forget."

"Oh. Yeah...I'll ask the pilot."

Lev was impressed by Irina's enthusiasm, but he also had some doubts. Despite the fact that the skills she needed to learn were for her own safety, she still struck him as maybe *too* eager. He'd always thought it was strange that she never complained about anything and never tried to escape; he wondered whether it was possible that she was lulling him into a false sense of security.

As Lev watched Irina fold the parachute, the echo of her lonely voice as she looked at Lilitto from the plane flashed across his mind. Maybe her family had been taken hostage, or she'd made a deal to sacrifice herself to save another person.

The UZSR would do anything to achieve its goals. After Gergiev seized power, the suppression and purging of dissenting voices had decreased in the name of the Zirnitra Union being a "peace-loving nation." Nevertheless, Delivery Crews worked behind the scenes, as they had always had.

"What's got you so grim?" Irina asked, catching Lev lost in thought.

"I, uh... I'm just tired," he replied.

"How pathetic when I've still got all this energy."

There was no doubt that Irina was putting up a front, but seeing her act so determined and cheerful brought a grin to Lev's face. He'd always worried about whether to ask her how she became a test subject. He had a feeling that, if the reason was something bad—something he could sympathize with—it'd affect his ability to make the necessary decisions as her supervisor.

He said nothing, maintaining the distance between them, and they repeated the high-altitude jump. The harder Lev tried to ignore it, however, the deeper Irina gradually embedded herself in his heart.

In November, about a month after Lev and Irina first met, her launch date was finally chosen.

"The site will be the Albinar Cosmodrome," Lev told Irina, who'd only just woken up. "The launch will be three weeks from now—December twelfth at 0504 hours."

The moment she heard the news, her eyes darkened resolutely. "Finally, a launch date."

She kept a stiff upper lip as Lev continued. "After breaking through the atmosphere and entering orbit, you'll fly through zero gravity for six minutes at twenty-eight thousand kilometers an hour. You'll do a lap around the Earth in about one hour and fifty minutes, then land in the desert near the base. Our job now is to make sure you can do a solo parachute landing before December twelfth."

Irina nodded, nervousness beginning to show on her face. "Right."

Until now, they'd erred on the side of caution, so Irina had yet to do a solo jump. They'd been afraid she might injure herself, which would cancel the launch entirely.

"Speaking of which," Lev added, "an important package arrived from Sangrad today."

"An important package?"

"Your space suit."

Five developers from a scientific manufacturing company had arrived at the Training Center with a complete space suit so Irina could try it on and check the size.

Lev and Irina found themselves looking at a set of equipment neither had ever seen before. It included a helmet that covered the entire head, a blue pressure suit made of durable synthetic elastic, and a bright orange space suit shell.

As the pair gasped in admiration, a scruffy developer told them about the space suit. "This equipment's pressure resistant and airtight. The shell color is intentionally eye-catching, so the test subject will be easily spotted if it lands in snow."

Although Lev wouldn't be wearing the suit himself, his heart raced with excitement, and he felt his palms begin to sweat. Perhaps sensing Lev's delight, Irina picked up the helmet and showed it to him. "It's really heavy."

"Not even the cosmonaut candidates have worn one of these before."

Irina giggled. "That makes me the first!"

She smiled boldly as the space suit fitting began. Since it was impossible to put the suit on by herself, the developers assisted her. Lev watched, something like impatience needling him. As a reserve, his future was still uncertain, but Irina would soon take to the skies.

"Phew! Is that everything?"

Wrapped in the baggy pressure suit and shell, with her sturdy helmet covering her head, Irina felt fully prepared. Still, the developers surrounded her to run checks on the twenty-kilogram space suit.

"How's it feel to wear?" one asked.

"It's heavy and tough to move in. And hot, like a sauna."

"That's because the space suit's airtight," the developer responded. Perhaps because he disliked Irina's answer, his voice grew harsh. "You'll just have to get used to that because you're going to an extreme environment. And keep in mind that you'll wear your space suit during your parachute jump upon your return to Earth."

The developers ordered Irina to do several tasks in succession while fully suited: jumping thirty times, stretching fifty times, running as fast as possible. Irina moved as best she could. Lev felt a little sorry for her, but kept his cool and watched in silence.

When the developers finished checking the space suit, it was immediately removed, without any chance for Irina to rest. Her skin and undergarments were visible under her sweat-drenched clothes, but she was so fatigued that she didn't even notice.

"That was harder than I thought," she said.

"Mm-hmm. Yeah, it looked that way." Lev averted his gaze, unable to look at Irina directly.

Catching a glimpse of herself in the mirror, Irina let out a short, high-pitched squeal. She crouched to hide herself, glaring at Lev. "You were staring at me!"

"I-I was not! You've got it all wrong!" Lev panicked.

Irina bared her fangs at him, her face reddening. "You call yourself my supervisor, so where's my change of clothes?!"

Irina went into the bathroom to get changed, leaving Lev to wait outside. There, he thought about his own destiny. Korovin had said, "I expect great things in your future," but that alone was no guarantee that Lev would be repromoted from reserve to full cosmonaut candidate.

It wasn't clear what would happen to Irina post-launch either. Dogs that safely and successfully returned to Earth lived out their days peacefully as researchers gathered data from them long-term. Did that mean Lev would be obliged to live his life in a solitary cell, supervising Irina indefinitely? His stomach tightened at the thought.

He wasn't sure how many sighs he heaved before he noticed the sound of shoes approaching down the corridor. He looked up to see Roza in her jogging suit, her expression irritated.

"I hear they fitted the vampire for a space suit," Roza said.

"Well, yeah. It was too big, though."

"And I hear the vampire's taken to training very conscientiously." Roza's words weren't a compliment; there was venom in them, as if she wanted to say more.

"Yeah, she's doing her best." Lev meant for his half-hearted answer to move Roza along.

Roza didn't move, however. Instead, her eyes filled with suspicion. "That vampire's planning something. Maybe it's a spy for the UK."

"No way. I've been watching since the start, and she's never done anything remotely suspicious. Plus, you know they would've done strict background checks on her family even before she got here."

"You trust it."

Lev hedged. "I'm just doing my duty."

"Your duty...?" Roza crossed her arms, looking annoyed. "Don't you think it's humiliating to be beaten by a vampire? To let one of *them* get up there first?"

"I'd be lying if I said I wasn't jealous. But humiliated? No."

Roza shook her head, seemingly unable to believe what she was hearing. "You're as guileless as they come. Then again, you *are* just a reserve. Maybe you lack the drive to be first."

It was clear Roza was jealous that Irina was being sent to space first—and also clear that, when Irina first introduced herself at the cafeteria, Roza had been gazing harshly at someone she saw as a rival.

"Hmph! It's not that it matters to me." Roza chuckled derisively. There was cruel ice in her voice as she continued. "Even if the vampire makes it back safely, it'll be disposed of when the experiments are done, like it never existed."

"Disposed of?" Uncertainty clawed at Lev's heart.

"Please do try to keep up. Unlike a dog, this test subject can talk. You think they'll just set it free? They'll nip it in the bud well before it can bloom into a problem for the UZSR."

Lev had no counterargument. However he looked at it, there was no bright future ahead for Irina as long as the UZSR remained a fearsome world power. Zirnitran officials definitely wouldn't just let her return to her hometown with a pat on the back and a friendly "Thanks for all your hard work!"

"Such a tragedy," Roza added. "It's working so hard, yet it's destined for death."

"Watch your mouth, Roza."

"Do you think the vampire's trying to impress the higher-ups so it can beg for mercy later? 'I'll keep being useful! Just don't kill me!' That kind of thing?"

"You wouldn't ask that if you saw how hard she works." Lev heard a slight growl in his tone. "She's putting everything into this."

Roza didn't back down. "Look at you covering for it. It hasn't bitten you, has it? Are you one of them now? Or have you just been seduced by the vampire's charms after spending all that time alone together?"

Lev couldn't hold back his anger. "Grow up, Roza! You think she's that kind of person?! She isn't!"

Roza's eyes widened. "'Person'? That's how you look at it?"

"Huh?" Lev had blurted out the word, and now that Roza confronted him with that fact, he couldn't hide his hesitation. "So I used the wrong word! It's not as if that even matters!"

As Lev tried to cover himself, Roza stared contemptuously. "You're a reserve because you're too nice and you don't think things through. You know a test subject from the cursed species should be treated the same as any other test animal—like an object."

Lev scratched the back of his head. That *was* exactly how he was supposed to act as a cosmonaut candidate. "I know my own weaknesses," he replied. "They're painfully clear to me. But that 'cursed species' thing is just awful, stupid discrimination. Don't you dare use those words again."

"Fine, fine..." Roza shrugged and then looked toward the bathroom entrance.

Lev felt a presence as well and turned to see Irina holding her dirty clothes. "Er..." He struggled to find the words to explain the situation.

Irina walked briskly toward Roza and stood in front of her. "If you have something you want to say to me, how about you say it to my face?" She gazed up at the cosmonaut candidate sharply.

Roza didn't back off. She simply raised her nose and looked down at Irina. "Even if your launch succeeds, I'll never acknowledge it as spaceflight."

"I never wanted your acknowledgment in the first place, human."

"I don't like your tone, vampire."

Icy sparks flew between the two young women's eyes, and a volatile aura sprang up around them.

"Calm down, both of you!" Lev hurried between the pair, although it felt like jumping into a wild animal's cage. He pulled Irina further from Roza.

"Hmph! Careful not to die out there, vampire," Roza snapped. "Make sure you don't get bitten, Lev." With that, she left.

Irina glared daggers at Roza's back, grinding her teeth.

"Did you, uh...did you hear all that?" Lev asked timidly.

"Only some of it," Irina said, pouting and scratching her head.

Although Lev was worried that Irina might've heard Roza throwing around phrases like "it'll be disposed of" and "destined for death," he couldn't bring himself to ask her. He didn't know what he'd do if Irina had questions about Roza's predictions. He also couldn't stand the awkward silence, so he decided to downplay the conversation. "Don't worry about Roza. She's always been aggressive and arrogant, no matter who she's with. And your being female probably pushed it up a notch."

Irina turned toward Lev, locking her gaze on him. "And just how do you feel about me, Lev?"

"Huh?" Lev's jaw dropped. The question had come out of left field.

The vampire girl hurriedly waved her hands. "Don't get the wrong idea—I don't mean anything weird!" she exclaimed, panicked. "But we've been together this long, and you've never asked me about myself. I just wondered."

Lev had kept an intentional distance; he was always aware that Irina might be killed during the launch. He couldn't tell her that, though, so he went with a different reply. "Um...I feel like you're really doing your best, considering that you were brought here against your will."

"Against my will?" said Irina, confused. "Who told you that?"

"Hm? Uh...nobody. I just assumed." Lev peered at her, gauging her reaction.

She looked upward for a moment, as if unsure whether she should speak, then went ahead. "You're wrong, then. There were other candidates too. I volunteered."

"You volunteered?" A shock ran through Lev. His guess had been entirely wrong. Now he saw why Irina approached her training so resolutely. "They're not coercing you into doing any of this?"

"What're you talking about? How would they?"

"Like, by...taking your family hostage, for example?"

Panic and confusion flashed across Irina's gaze for a moment, but she shook her head emphatically. "Unbelievable. No. Could you please *not* make up bizarre stories about me?"

"Sorry..."

"Whatever. It's fine. Let's go." Irina turned away, heading toward the training rooms.

From the atmosphere, it was clear that family wasn't a topic Irina wanted to get into. But Lev couldn't let it go. On one hand, Irina had volunteered as a test subject...but on the other, Lev had noticed how she looked away from her hometown aboard the trainer. He wondered exactly what burden she carried.

"Maybe she ran away from home?" he murmured.

Lev swallowed his curiosity. He had a hunch that, if he asked, Irina would only close herself off again.

During the next training session, Irina was as conscientious as always. Seeing her so diligent, Lev felt a little relieved; it seemed highly unlikely that she'd heard Roza mention "disposing of" the test subject. Still, the words stuck in Lev's mind. They needled his heart with a lingering sting every time he spoke to Irina.

In late November, LAIKA44 was wrapped in arctic winds that people often called "the breath of Moroz." The cold soaked into one's core. The snow-capped trees lining the streets looked as if they wore white hats, and thick ice covered the artificial lake. It was the beginning of a long, harsh winter.

Lev was reading Irina the next week's schedule. He had wrapped himself in a thick military coat to bear the chilly, isolated cells, but Irina seemed perfectly fine in her usual jacket.

"At the beginning of next week, you'll do solitude training in the anechoic altitude chamber."

When Lev mentioned a type of training Irina had never heard of, she furrowed her brow. "That sounds suspicious. What is it?"

"An airtight space with high oxygen and low pressure."

Nothing was audible outside the anechoic altitude chamber, and the walls themselves absorbed all sound—there was never an echo. During training, a candidate fitted with sensors was left alone in the chamber for an unspecified number of days. They could contact those outside via radio at assigned times, but they'd receive no response.

"What's the point of that kind of training?" Irina asked.

"The cabin a cosmonaut rides in is completely isolated. One reason for anechoic altitude chamber training is to adjust to that unique solitude. It also simulates the environment you might experience if a spaceflight encountered an unexpected situation or problem. Getting to space is one thing, but if there's some issue, there's a chance you might be trapped there for a long time. All we can do is...pray that doesn't happen."

Lev felt awkward explaining that part to Irina. You could warn someone about it, but they still wouldn't be able to escape. If it occurred, it would be fatal.

As Irina learned more about the training, her expression grew somber. "How long will I be stuck in the room for?"

"All they tell you is that it's more than one day and fewer than ten. But once the door unlocks, it's over."

Irina sighed, playing with a strand of hair absentmindedly.

Just imagining the anechoic altitude chamber was probably depressing. Even Lev liked that type of training least.

"Solitude will be mentally grueling, so you have tomorrow off," Lev concluded. "If there's someplace you want to go, I recommend we take time to do it, so you can clear your head. I mean, uh...as your supervisor, I'll have to come along. Still, if you want to go somewhere..." Lev found himself struggling with the words; he wasn't used to inviting girls out.

Irina was silent. She stared at Lev for a while. Then her gaze darted around nervously, and she started playing with her hair again.

At a loss for what to do, Lev fidgeted pointlessly with his coat buttons. "Er...if, uh...if you don't want to go somewhere, you don't have to," he added anxiously.

"Where do *you* go on days off?" asked Irina, still toying with her locks and avoiding his eyes.

"Me? Uh...I guess I usually go to a jazz bar."

"Then let's do that."

"What?"

Irina still wouldn't look at him. "I said, let's go to a...jazz bar."

The suggestion blindsided Lev completely. "Do you like jazz?"

"Hm?"

"It's just, you said you don't drink, so..."

"No, it's... Well, don't...don't get the wrong idea. I..." Irina continued to fiddle.

Seeing her hesitation, Lev decided he should make sure she knew what she was in for. "The jazz bar's crowded on weekends. Are you all right with that?"

"Um...crowded?"

From Irina's responses, Lev grasped the source of the confusion. "You don't actually know what a jazz bar is, do you?"

Irina pouted, making no attempt to reply. When Lev didn't speak, her cheeks flushed red.

"You don't, do you?" Lev finally repeated.

Irina bit her lip but still didn't answer.

"Well, they have drinks besides alcohol. You can always just sit back and enjoy the music," Lev continued. "But I have to ask, why a ja—"

"Enough questions! Just take me, all right?!" Irina turned away and got into her coffin, slamming the lid closed.

"Er..."

Until now, Irina had avoided human contact whenever possible. What'd come over her? Lev burned with curiosity. Under the circumstances, however, it didn't look as if he'd get an answer anytime soon.

"I guess the two of us are...going to Zvezda." Just imagining it stirred up butterflies in Lev's stomach.

The next day, Lev and Irina headed to the bar. Lev wore his off-duty leather jacket and slacks; Irina wore her winter cap to cover her ears, her necklace, and a black poncho that went all the way to her knees. They walked along sidewalks starting to pile with light snow, heading for Jazz Bar Zvezda.

Lev was used to seeing Irina in plain gym clothes or an oppressive military uniform; there was something new and refreshing about her big poncho. "I think this is the first time we've been out in casual clothes," he said.

"It feels awkward."

"Yeah. Yeah, it does."

A long silence filled the air. Eventually, he tried to break it. "Uh...it sure is cold out, huh?"

"Not really."

Another awkward silence washed over the pair. Lev, lost for words, kicked absently at fallen pinecones while Irina stared at the smoke rising from the chimneys. They entered the residential sector quietly, then arrived at the commercial district, which was beginning to light up with neon.

Mikhail and three other cosmonaut candidates happened to be passing by. Mikhail waved when he noticed Lev and Irina, but there was no smile on his face. "Fancy seeing you here. Where are you headed?"

Lev was secretly relieved that something had broken the long silence. "Zvezda. You?"

Mikhail mimed hitting a ball across a pool table. "Billiards." He turned to Irina. "I hear you had a spat with Roza."

"I didn't stoop to *that* level," Irina replied, apparently hoping to end the conversation there.

Mikhail and the other candidates looked at each other and laughed.

"Something funny?" asked Irina.

Lev didn't want to get into an argument on the outskirts of the residential sector; this whole conversation was unnecessary to begin with. Sliding between Irina and the cosmonaut candidates, he tapped her shoulder, telling Mikhail, "We'll be on our way, then."

As he and Irina turned to leave, however, Mikhail eyed them with a cruel smile. "We expect big things from your launch."

Lev just waved half-heartedly and pulled Irina along.

"He's a creep," Irina muttered.

"Ignore it. They're jealous."

Lev did feel ostracized by the cosmonaut candidate circle, but he had absolutely no desire to rejoin them if it'd mean treating Irina heartlessly.

When Lev opened the door to Jazz Bar Zvezda, he and Irina were met with light jazz music and wafting cigarette smoke.

Irina looked around curiously; her eyes rested on the phonograph and speaker. "Are the sounds coming from that spinning disc?"

"It's called a record," said Lev. Genuine vinyl records circulated in LAIKA44, although the records floating around other areas were much lower quality, since they were made from discarded x-ray photographs.

"I've never heard this type of music before." Lilitto was high in the mountains, where radio waves didn't reach; its musical culture had never left the Middle Ages.

"Jazz comes from a culture within the UK, so it was banned here for ages," Lev explained. "They only recently relented and let people listen to it. What do you think?"

Irina stood tall and listened carefully. Her face softened. "It sounds nice."

"I'm really glad you like it! Let's get something to drink. What're you having, milk?"

Irina looked at the menu. "Given the occasion, I guess I'll have a...lemon seltzer, just for you."

Lev chuckled. "Got it." He ordered a lemon seltzer and a nastoyka, then carried the drinks and some bready snacks to their stools at the end of the counter. "Here's to your hard work."

Their glasses came together with a clink.

Irina smelled the lemon seltzer, then allowed herself a sip. After savoring it for a while, she took a second gulp. "It's good," she said finally. "But I wish it wasn't." As she smiled, her eyes narrowed slightly, and her fangs peeked from her mouth.

Seeing her smile for the first time startled Lev. "Oh..." She had a young girl's pure, innocent smile. For a moment, his eyes and heart were completely taken by it.

"What is it this time?" Irina tilted her head. "I just praised your favorite drink, didn't I?"

"It's nothing," Lev said, adding, "Human drinks aren't so bad after all, right?" He sipped his nastoyka, hoping Irina wouldn't notice his face turning pink.

"What're you drinking?" she asked. "It's a beautiful red."

"This is a fruit liqueur made by steeping silverberries in zhizni for three weeks. I like it with a secret ingredient—cotton-thistle honey." Irina nodded, intrigued. Lev wondered what'd happen if she drank; he felt his playful side stir again. "Do you want to try a little?"

"I told you, I'm only seventeen."

"Maybe Lilitto's legal drinking age is twenty, but here in Zirnitra, you can drink from sixteen. As the saying goes, 'Don't visit a monastery and bring your own rulebook.'"

"Hmm..." Lev could see that Irina was on the fence.

He gave her a little push. "You could discover a brand-new taste, like when you tried soda water. You never know."

"Fine. I'll have one sip." Taking Lev's glass, Irina drank a little nastoyka. Her eyes widened in agitation. "My tongue! My mouth! Fire!" She scrambled to gulp her lemon seltzer.

Lev burst into laughter. "Not what you expected?"

"It tastes like disinfectant! Ew..." Irina waved her face to cool it. "I think I might be too young to drink that."

Lev felt a little bad about the prank. "Get a glass of milk to help wash it down, maybe?"

"Is soda milk served here?"

"Uh, no." Just imagining that turned Lev's stomach.

Irina seemed to enjoy the jazz; her body rocked gently in time with the piano and brass section. Lev felt it'd be rude to distract her with conversation, so he sat back with his glass in hand and sipped the time away. Passersby glanced at Irina occasionally, their eyes drawn by an unusual beauty who didn't suit the smoke-filled bar. A few of the voices floating around asked who the young woman was. Lev felt proud to have brought a beautiful girl to Zvezda for the first time, yet it was also odd to think that he was out drinking with a vampire.

"What's this song?" Irina asked.

"It's called 'My Beloved.'"

"I really like it—although I don't understand the lyrics. It's in a foreign language, isn't it?"

Lev was a few drinks deep and comfortably tipsy, which made it easier to break his own rules around talking about Irina's origins. "Back in Lilitto, what'd you do on days off?"

"Hm? Why do you ask?" Irina's words were slightly slurred, and her cheeks had turned light pink. She'd only drunk a little, but she was tipsy too.

"I don't know. Just curious."

Irina put a finger to her jaw. "Read books, took care of plants, looked after cows and goats," she replied, seemingly traipsing through memories with each example.

"That's like something right out of a pastoral storybook."

"Well, there wasn't anything else to do. What about you, Lev? What'd you do before you came to LAIKA44?"

In contrast to Irina's warm, gentle tone, Lev spoke somberly. "I was always flying the skies."

"The skies...?"

"I was an air force pilot before getting here. In university, I was part of the local aviation club. And when I was little, I built my own planes and hurt myself flying them off the roof." Saying it aloud made him feel as though he really had lived life in the sky.

"You must've been strange," Irina giggled. The ice in her glass was melting; she took another sip and then turned back to Lev. "So when did you decide you wanted to go to space?"

"Long before I even wanted to fly a plane."

Clear scenes from old memories floated into Lev's mind. "When I was five, I saw a fighter jet pass a crescent moon. I wondered if I could fly all the way to the moon in a plane like that. In retrospect, it was a silly thought. But I honestly decided then that I'd do it one day—go to the moon, then Mars and Venus."

"Hmm." Irina listened intently, watching Lev with passion in her eyes.

"I decided to join the air force after I met the teacher I told you about."

"The one who said aircraft aren't weapons?"

"Yeah." Drinking the last of his nastoyka, Lev gripped the glass tightly. The old indignation once more ignited in his heart, lending power to his voice. "I thought that if the war ended, the world would change. And the world really is changing, although there are still regional disputes. That's why I'll never come to terms with my teacher's fate. Abducted for telling the truth! Why? Space rockets *aren't* weapons for destroying the UK! They should be symbols of peace!"

"Bit loud, don't you think?" The voice—accompanied by a pat on Lev's shoulder—was one Lev had heard before.

"Huh?!" He whipped around, shocked.

The dorm matron, Natalia, stood behind him. At first, Lev didn't recognize her without her usual kerchief and apron. If she hadn't been wearing her glasses, she might've looked like an entirely different person.

"N-Natalia?!" he stammered. "What're you doing here?"

Natalia showed him the near-empty mug in her hand. "Even I come to Zvezda for a drink or two on occasion. Or are you saying my place is in the cafeteria, making soup?"

"Uh, no, of course not. Sorry. I was just surprised." *I guess even the dorm matron has another side,* Lev thought, before realizing that was obvious.

Natalia sighed, exasperated. She leaned close to Lev and whispered in his ear. "Anyway, I'm all for passionate speeches, but shouldn't you watch out for the Delivery Crew? If you keep ranting about the UK, you'll paint a target on your back."

"Oh." Lev suddenly realized he'd risen from his seat. He sat down quietly and awkwardly scratched the back of his head, glancing at Irina. "Sorry." It was a mixed blessing that he could be passionate and invisible simultaneously.

"You're such a pain," Natalia tutted. Irina cracked a wry grin, and the dorm matron looked at her sympathetically. "This can't be easy for you, Irina. Aren't you getting tired of Snow Thaw Lev?"

"'Snow Thaw'…?"

"If he gets talking about flying or space, he's so fiery he'll melt any snow or ice nearby—or so they say."

Irina rested her head on her hand, peering at Lev. "You know I'm not good with heat, right?" she joked.

Lev felt himself shrink under the women's jibes. "All right, all right. I said I'm sorry."

"I have to ask, Lev," Natalia continued. "You brought Irina to a bar—you're not getting her tipsy so you can make a pass at her, are you?"

"I'd never do that! Why do you always say that kind of thing?"

"Why? Well, during Irina's checkup, I distinctly remember you claiming that the door was cool and—"

"Ah! Ah-ah-ah!" Lev yelped the moment he realized Natalia might reveal that he'd eavesdropped, which drew the attention of all the other patrons.

Natalia raised a finger to her lips. "As I said before—bit loud, don't you think?"

"Yes, but..." Lev shot a glance in Irina's direction.

He was confronted by her suspicious gaze. "The door was cool?"

"I-It was nothing. Nothing at all. Right, Natalia?" Lev shot the dorm matron a pleading gaze.

Natalia smiled. "The doors *are* cold during the winter. Well, I'll leave you two to it. Bye." She finished her beer and walked off.

Lev sighed. He'd had such a nice buzz going, only to be ripped back into reality. He looked at his watch; since it was nearing nine at night, he thought a change of scenery might be in order. Now that he'd gotten too rowdy twice already, he felt a little uncomfortable lingering at the bar.

"What do you want to do next?" he asked Irina.

"What else is there to do?"

"Well, we could see a movie." He caught himself before telling Irina that the theater ran movies all night. This week, he remembered, a special collection of vampire films was showing. It'd be torture to make Irina watch a film about a hunter tracking vampires weak to crucifixes and garlic. "Actually, going to a movie would just make us sleepy. How about..."

He hesitated. He'd always followed the rules and gotten back to the dormitory before curfew, so he wasn't too familiar with LAIKA44's nightlife. There were no soccer matches this late at night, and if they went to play billiards, they were bound to run into other cosmonaut candidates. That left only one thing. "Ah, I've got it! How about skating?"

"Skating?"

"There's a frozen lake on the outskirts of town. Do you know how to skate?"

Irina looked suddenly interested. "I'm quite good at it."

"Well, how about it?"

"I don't have skates." Her shoulders drooped.

"I'll buy you a pair." Lev raised a finger in the air. "The department store near here sells them, and it's still open!"

Irina shook her head. "I don't want to owe you." She was fidgeting, though. Lev could tell that she was being stubborn and that she really wanted to go skate.

"Consider it part of training," he replied. "Cosmonaut candidates are paid pretty well, you know. And I just keep saving money because there's nothing to spend it on."

"Aren't you a *reserve* cosmonaut candidate?" Irina objected. "Do you even get paid?"

"Quiet, you! Let's go."

Lev bought them two pairs of skates, and they headed to the lake at the edge of LAIKA44.

"Why'd you buy skates for yourself?" asked Irina.

"Just sitting around watching you skate would be pretty boring, wouldn't it? And if I don't keep moving, I'll probably freeze to death." As he spoke, the breath of Moroz sent a gust of chilly wind at them, as though on cue. Lev took out a flask of zhizni, drinking a little to warm his body up. "*Brr.* Sure is cold."

"You're drinking too much." Irina rolled her eyes, slightly annoyed.

"When it's a guy's day off, go easy on him, all right? To citizens of the UZSR, zhizni's no different from water," Lev insisted. "We aren't all blessed with cold resistance like you."

They bantered and chattered, finally nearing the lake. After trudging through soft snow that came up to their ankles, they arrived at the shore. The ice across the lake's surface shone with brilliant white light, reflecting the moon.

"It looks like we've got the whole lake to ourselves," said Irina.

"Well, on a night as cold as tonight, you'd have to be a real weirdo to come out here to skate."

"So you're a weirdo, then."

"I'm here as your supervisor!"

They cleared snow from a nearby bench and put on their new ice skates. Although Lev was hiding it, he was full of an excitement that reminded him of sneaking into an empty school building in the middle of the night.

"Since there's nobody here, I can take off my cap, right?" Removing her hat, Irina glided across the ice eagerly.

Lev followed, but he could barely stay upright in his inebriated state. "Ugh...maybe I really *did* drink a bit too much."

A smile crept onto Irina's face as she watched him. "Race?"

"Huh?"

"Whoever makes it to the far shore and back fastest wins!" Before she finished the sentence, she was already skating along the ice.

"Hey! Wait!" Lev slipped and almost tumbled down, but he managed to keep his balance at the last moment. "Phew! That was close."

He tried to chase Irina, but his body wouldn't listen to him—he couldn't skate straight. On the other hand, Irina seemed completely sober. She skated gracefully, humming "My Beloved," which she apparently remembered from Jazz Bar Zvezda.

Lev somehow kept his balance all the way to the shore and back, although he couldn't count how many times he almost fell.

Back at their starting point, Irina had a hand on one hip. "You were so slow, I was about to doze off," she said, making a great show of yawning.

"I'd never have skated like this...if I hadn't been drinking." Lev's head spun from the sudden bout of intoxicated exercise. "How about...resting a little?"

He sat on the bench again, leaning back and staring blankly at Irina. Her hair flowed behind her as she skated across the ice.

The moon followed and illuminated her like a spotlight; the bits of ice that billowed behind her skates were like glittering stardust. To Lev's dizzy, exhausted eyes, it was a fantastic sight. It was like watching a sprightly snow fairy carve a magic seal on the lake—like a secret, sacred ritual. Lev was utterly charmed. He forgot the freezing cold and even the passing of time.

Irina danced exuberantly upon the ice of the silent lake. She seemed to be momentarily free from suffocating reality—to be living in, and enjoying, the moment. As thin clouds veiled the moon, the fairy waltz ended.

"That was so much fun!"

Irina sat down next to Lev. Her forehead had broken into a light sweat, and her cheeks were red as apples. Had her hair been any wetter, it would've frozen solid. Without anything specific to talk about, the two simply stared up at the night sky. The vast, boundless portrait of the heavens above seemed to stretch for an eternity.

"It's hard to believe we'll fly all the way out there," Lev muttered, almost as if he were talking to himself.

"You mean, reserves will get to fly there too?" Irina grinned cheekily.

"No... I, uh...I mean..." Lev didn't want to say he *wouldn't* go to space, but he couldn't find the right response.

"You told me you had pretty good grades, didn't you? How'd you end up a reserve?"

Lev wondered for a moment whether he should tell her. He realized there was nothing to hide. "I was demoted for attacking a superior."

"*You* attacked a superior?!"

Bitter memories floated back, and he clenched his teeth. "The son of the Fourth Design Bureau Chief treated new engineers like his personal slaves. He blamed one for a failure that wasn't their fault and told them they were fired. While they knelt on the floor, apologizing, he stepped on them. He'd always acted that way, but I just couldn't stand it. Before I knew it, I'd hit him."

Irina nodded knowingly. "You're so fiery. I guess they don't call you Snow Thaw Lev for nothing."

"Agh, just drop the nickname." Still embarrassed, Lev scratched the back of his head, and regret crawled through his body; he'd raised a hand against a superior. He tried to put it out of his mind with another swig of zhizni.

"How do you drink that stuff? It sets your mouth on fire!"

"How about when you turn twenty, you give it one more try?" Lev suggested.

Irina seemed suddenly lost for words. Looking down at her feet, she packed together a small pile of snow beneath them. "If... if I live that long, I'll toast my birthday with some zhizni." Her voice wavered, and her lips trembled; the end of the sentence seemed to disappear into the wind.

"Wait. Why 'if you live that long'?"

Lev felt the air change as Irina turned to him with a forced smile. "Test subjects end up disposed of, right? Killed, basically?"

A chill went down his spine. "You heard what Roza said, didn't you?"

"Roza *and* you. You're both so loud."

Lev simply couldn't believe she'd overheard them. After he'd talked with Roza outside the bathroom, he'd watched Irina go about her training as if nothing had changed.

"This country's horrific, isn't it?" Irina asked, seemingly trying to stay strong.

He didn't have the faintest idea what to say to her. It wasn't as if he could just end the conversation by suggesting they head back to the cells. He felt a weight in the pit of his stomach and a cold that reached the bottom of his heart.

The powder snow danced whimsically in the air; some settled on the back of his hand, where it melted and vanished.

"An aurora..." Irina's whisper echoed gently through the heavy silence that draped over the lake shore.

Lev lifted his head and saw a jade-green curtain sway against the glittering stars of the night sky. Wrapped in melancholic shadow, Irina raised a finger and traced the aurora's edges.

"In my village," she told Lev, "they say the aurora is a bridge to the world of the dead." Lev waited for her to go on. "Your teacher said that aircraft aren't weapons," she continued. "If all humans thought like that, perhaps my village wouldn't have burned to the ground."

"Hm?"

Irina's hand moved silently into a gesture of prayer in front of her chest. "When I was three years old, my parents were pulled into the war and killed."

"Oh no..." Lev felt heartsick, and words suddenly failed him.

"They hid me under the dressing table," Irina went on calmly, holding back her emotions with each word. "My mother was stabbed through the heart, and my father was decapitated. I saw it with my own eyes. So many villagers died. The castle was torn down, and the attackers set fire to the forests. They didn't even spare the livestock." She held the jewel on her necklace gently in her hands. "As I watched the forest burn, I couldn't stop wondering why this had to happen to us. I stayed in the castle cellars by myself, reading old books, hoping to find an answer, for so many long years..." Her eyes grew damp.

There was nothing Lev could say to make things better. His grip on the flask of zhizni tightened.

"But that was a long time ago. Forget I said anything." Irina wiped tears from the corners of her eyes and then forced an awkward smile. "Oh—that reminds me. Do you know the legend that vampires are the 'People of the Moon'?"

The question surprised Lev, but he sensed her desire to change the subject, so he went along with it. "Yes. I really believed that as a kid, you know."

"I used to think it was just another legend," Irina continued. "But when I saw the satellite photo of the dark side of the moon that the newspaper published, I couldn't believe my eyes. It looked just like pictures my ancestors drew in the sixteenth century."

"Huh? What're you getting at?"

Irina shook her head sadly. "They're just sketches in old, moldy manuscripts, and nobody understands the text alongside them—it's like a code. Still, that photo proved something to me.

Vampires *are* the People of the Moon. We belong there, and that's why we're oppressed down here."

She took off her necklace, lifting the jewel toward the sky. "Lunny kamen. It's a moonstone passed down through generations." Caught in the light of the moon, the gem shone a subtle blue that brightened with the aurora's movements.

"Sinus Iridum...Lacus Somniorum...Palus Somni," Irina uttered, voice clear, as her jewel captured the moonlight. "Oceanus Procellarum...Mare Vaporum..."

The Poem of the Moon sounded like a pained prayer, and it sank into Lev's heart.

"Tenerife Massif...Palus Putredinis..." Under the moon, the wind lifted Irina's hair high, as if reacting to her words. "Sinus Fluctus...Promontorium Laplace..."

As her solemn poem ended, Irina silently held the stone in her palm, staring at it. "I want to take this to the moon." She paused, clasping the gem to her chest. "But I don't have wings, so I can't fly like the vampires in legends. In my village deep in the mountains, without planes or technology, all I could do was pray. Eventually, I met humans from Zirnitra."

Moonlight shined in Irina's eyes as she stared upward. They were bright red, as if her passion were concealed within them. "I don't care about being a test subject, and I don't mind using human equipment," she said. "I just want to reach the moon."

The purity of Irina's hopes touched Lev's heart. This was why she'd never once complained during training and why she always did the very best she could. She had a will of steel and stronger motivation than any cosmonaut candidate.

On her first day, when she'd stood before the monument and looked at the night sky, Lev was sure that Irina had been full of these very thoughts. He'd never known any of this—never realized her hidden feelings—and he was ashamed of having thought that she had ulterior motives.

Irina kept her eyes on the sky above. "If I make it back safely from space, perhaps I *will* be disposed of, but that's fine." Her words were like a resolution she'd carved into her heart. "If I kept living in the mountains, I'd never reach my dreams. I want to visit space before any human and see it before they can sully it." There were tears in her eyes as she stared at the sky, holding back the tremble in her voice. "So, please, stay with me a little longer."

"Of course," Lev said. "Whatever happens, I'm on your side." He couldn't do much more than help her train, but he wanted to see her dream come true.

"Thank you, Lev." As the powder snow fell, it danced in the wind like stardust, melting on Irina's cheeks. Irina stood, a sorrowful smile on her face. "I'm going to skate a little more."

Lev watched her silhouette walk onto the ice, his fingers opening his flask of zhizni. He took a sip and felt his throat burn while warmth coursed to the core of his body.

интерлюдия

INDIGO EYES
• ОЧИ ИНДИГО •

I**N THE COSMODROME'S** launch control center—known as the "blockhouse"—Lev watched the monitor intently. At this very moment, in a darkness impenetrable by light, Irina's rocket was launching. Inside the cabin, Irina herself sat stock-still, as though she were a wax model. She'd closed her eyes.

Engineers' voices rang out around Lev.

"Engine ignition!"

"Main combustion chamber!"

"Firing engine!"

And then, "Launch!"

With that final order, the engines roared and the rocket began to take off—but a moment later, it tilted, burst into flames, and exploded.

The rumble of the explosion pierced Lev's ears, and the blockhouse walls shook wildly. The monitor went black. Rocket parts slammed against the blockhouse roof as panicked engineers and technicians ran around.

Lev stood locked in place, frozen with shock. "Aaahhh!"

A devastating tremor rocked the blockhouse. As the building's roof crumbled, the rocket's flaming cabin hurtled toward Lev's head, and—

"Augh!" Lev sat up suddenly. He was in bed in his cell. His forehead had broken into a sweat, and his heart felt like it was going to burst out of his chest. "A dream...?"

Sighing in relief, he looked at the wall that separated his cell from Irina's. Irina wasn't on the other side; she was in the anechoic altitude chamber for a five-day solitude training session. Lev was continuing his own training solo, dropping by periodically to check on her. There was no way to contact Irina directly while she was isolated from the outside world, so he could only get reports from Anya, who was supervising.

He'd last checked on Irina before he went to bed. She was working on math problems, but it was clear from her face that she was bored.

As he stared at Irina's image on the monitor, Anya had poked fun at him. "Someone's looking a bit deflated. So, you lose motivation without little Irinyan around?"

"Don't be silly. It's nice to finally have some time to myself."

That was Lev's claim, but it was true that he felt like something was missing from his life.

Even Franz brought it up when Lev went for hot room training. "You worried about her?"

"Yeah."

"She's cute," the engineer said, although his face was still serious.

"Wh-what're you talking about? I'm worried because I'm her *supervisor*!" Lev panicked. Franz walked straight to him and wrapped him in a hug, patting his back a few times. "Franz! What're you doing?!"

"I suspect the road ahead won't be easy," Franz whispered. "But do your best, all right?"

"Where...where'd that come from, all of a sudden?"

As he let Lev go, a gloomy smile appeared on Franz's face. "There's a chance I might have to leave LAIKA44."

Lev was shocked. "What?! Are you quitting?"

"No, it'd probably be more like a...transfer." There was a weight to his voice.

At that point, Lev remembered that Franz wasn't Vice-Director Sagalevich's biggest fan. "Is it the vice-director?" he asked. "Let me know if I can do anything to help."

"Forget it, Lev. Let's start your training." Franz pointed toward the hot room, busying himself with his usual tasks.

Lev thought there was something odd about the young man's behavior, but when the hot room training began, the sweat pouring from his body washed the feeling away.

SCARLET EYES
• ОЧИ АЛЫЙ •

TWO FULL DAYS had passed since Irina entered the anechoic altitude chamber. There were sensors all over her body, and the tape that held them firmly in place was getting itchy.

"I wish I could just tear them off already," Irina muttered. The chamber walls quickly absorbed her voice.

Irina couldn't pick up any sounds outside the chamber; all she heard was the quiet hum of the ventilation fan. Cans of beef and sardines, tubes of space food, and bottles of water were piled in one corner of the room. Overall, it was like being trapped in a bomb shelter. Although she'd spent most of her life alone, Irina could feel the mental strain of the solitude affecting her.

She sighed, deciding to return to finishing the tests she'd received to work on during the simulation. Before she could do so, however, the lights went out, blanketing Irina in darkness.

"Ack!" Despite her night vision, she couldn't see a thing. It was a total blackout.

With nothing else left to do, Irina stretched out on the floor. She felt as though her mind and body were melting into the darkness—as though the outside world could be destroyed completely, and she still wouldn't notice a thing.

"I wonder what Lev's doing now." The reserve cosmonaut candidate had been annoying at first. Now that they were almost always together, though, being apart felt lonely.

Lev had gotten genuinely angry at Roza, Irina remembered. It was irritating that he treated her like a human—she was a vampire, after all—but she was also glad to be seen as something other than a test subject, to be seen as a person.

She'd even had fun with Lev. She enjoyed skating, and she'd felt grown-up at the jazz bar. It was the kind of place she'd never have gone on her own. *When did my heart start to fill with these feelings?* she wondered.

"No," Irina grumbled, hands tousling her hair. "What am I thinking? I should be glad to finally be away from humans for a change."

Since being awake was only leading to pointless, vexing thoughts, Irina elected to go to sleep. When she closed her eyes, however, memories bubbled to the surface.

She remembered hiding under the dressing table and her parents' blood flowing. She remembered the cows she'd lovingly reared burning to death. She remembered her favorite dress, dirtied with mud and grime. She remembered lying in her cramped coffin, getting carried away imagining outer space and the unknown world of the moon. And she remembered being alone—always alone—as she stared up at the sky.

"Why did I tell him about that?" Her heart filled with sorrow and loneliness. Tears rose to her eyes and dripped down her cheeks. It was like a dam had burst.

"Please...please, don't turn the lights back on," Irina whispered, lying facedown on the floor. She didn't want a human to see her cry, especially not Lev.

CHAPTER 4

Blood Connection

INDIGO EYES
• ОЧИ ИНДИГО •

AFTER FIVE DAYS in the anechoic altitude chamber, Irina was finally released.

"Phew..." She slouched like an old, withered tree.

Lev was ready and waiting with a lemon seltzer. "Good work, Irina."

"Is that lemon seltzer?!" Irina beamed as she reached for the drink. Then, just as suddenly, her face grew stern. "You really thought this would cheer me up?"

"Huh?"

"I'll only drink this because it'd be a waste to dump it out." Irina snatched the cup from Lev's hand, taking a big gulp. "Mmm! This, uh, tastes awful."

"Uh-huh. Anyway, it must be nice to finally have those five days behind you."

"I never want to do that again," Irina replied. "You humans think up the most boring training. It makes me wonder how your brains were constructed in the first place."

For some reason, Lev felt relieved to hear her complain after so long.

Irina's eyes narrowed to slits. "What're you grinning about?"

Lev pretended nothing had happened, clearing his throat. "Well, um...from here on out, we'll prioritize parachute training. If we don't, you'll never master it in time for the launch."

After thinking long and hard about how to increase their chance of success, Lev had decided the best course of action would be practicing as much as possible, and he'd gotten Lt. Gen. Viktor's permission to revise Irina's schedule.

"As of today, we're putting study sessions and strength and endurance training on hold," he told Irina. "From 2200 hours, it'll all be parachute training. Once you finish your seltzer, we'll get straight to it!"

Candidates usually had a rest day after solitude training in the anechoic altitude chamber. With Irina's launch date fast approaching, though, Lev had to be strict.

Irina knew parachute training was her Achilles' heel, so she ignored her exhaustion and finished her lemon seltzer. "If I don't get better at landing, it'll be all your fault."

Over three days, they made thirty jumps. Irina no longer trembled with fear; she'd shown marked improvement. Now that she was comfortable with tandem jumps, it was time for her first solo jump.

It was a moonlit night, windy with the cold breath of Moroz, as their helicopter rose to maximum altitude above the military airfield. Irina sat at the open door, face hard and tight.

Lev put a reassuring hand on her shoulder. "It's all the same as a tandem jump. Position your arms and legs correctly to create wind resistance so you can control your descent. When the timing is right, open the drogue parachute and aim for your landing point. And don't look straight down!"

"G-got it!"

"Just relax. I'll be right there with you."

Irina looked into Lev's eyes and nodded, getting into exit posture. "Ready when you are!"

"All right! Three, two, one, go!" Lev pushed Irina from the helicopter, jumping out himself just moments later.

As they dropped into freefall, Lev took Irina's hand, his firm nod sending her a message: *You'll be all right.* Irina replied with an awkward smile, gripping his hand tight in return. She let go when it was time to open her parachute, and they moved far enough apart not to collide.

Lev gave Irina a thumbs-up: *Open your drogue parachute!* Pulling her rip cord, she went through the steps flawlessly. Lev breathed a sigh of relief, then followed suit and opened his own. The pair floated down to the landing point, Irina slightly above Lev.

Everything was going smoothly; she just had to nail the landing. There were no bodies of water around, so drowning wasn't a concern. There were no rocky outcrops to worry about either—only soft, grassy fields. As long as Irina did a proper five-point landing, there was no danger that she'd be seriously injured.

They neared the ground and took landing postures. Lev

touched down first. Rising quickly to his feet, he ran to where Irina would land.

"You can do it, Irina! Come on!" he shouted. "Five-point landing!"

Tension was written all over Irina's face, and her ankle twisted awkwardly as she hit the ground. Unable to break her fall properly, she rolled clumsily to a halt, then lay staring into the sky.

"Irina!" Lev shouted, running up to the girl.

He found her breathing heavily, but she smiled up at him, letting out a deep sigh of relief. "I landed."

Lev smiled back. "For a first solo jump, that was excellent," he said. "But that was just the first jump. Practice isn't over yet. If you find yourself trapped in spin, and you can't get clear quickly, you'll be in grave danger."

Throughout the entire jump procedure, "spin" was the state a cosmonaut had to be most careful of. As he released Irina from her parachute, Lev explained why it was so frightening.

Once a cabin reentered the atmosphere, there was a chance ejection might not go as planned, which could cause a cosmonaut's body to whirl at almost uncontrollably high speeds. That was what Lev meant by "spin." In that state, your eyes stung and the world looked blurry. Centrifugal force sent blood to your extremities, so your fingers felt like they'd rip off. Your head grew extremely heavy, and you lost all sense of direction.

"If you end up in spin, you need to stabilize your fall posture to ensure your parachute opens safely. In a worst-case scenario, you'll black out and plummet straight to Earth."

"Ugh..."

"I'm not trying to intimidate you, Irina. Next time we do a tandem jump, you'll get to feel spin for yourself." Just thinking about spin recovery gave Lev a headache, but he knew Irina had to personally experience it at least once.

The pair folded their parachutes and headed back to the airfield. As they did, Irina noticed something and pointed toward it. Far off in the sky, they saw the bright glow of a fireball streaking toward the ground.

"What's that, Lev? A shooting star, maybe?" Irina asked. "It's not an enemy attack, is it?"

Lev couldn't tell what it was either. "It's not a meteor. Is it a satellite?!"

The fireball drew closer, and Irina took a step backward. "Is it heading for us?!"

"No, but it'll land nearby."

Shooting over their heads, the fireball crashed with a heavy thud a few hundred meters from where they stood. The earth shook beneath them as the rough impact echoed in the night sky. Small flames flickered near the crash site.

"What do we do?" Irina asked.

Lev wasn't sure, but he decided that as a private second class, it was his responsibility to check into the fireball. "Let's go," he said.

They ran toward the crash site. As they saw the spot more clearly, their faces grew somber. At the center of a crater roughly twenty meters wide, the remains of a cabin were embedded in the ground. The cabin's silver exterior was scorched black, and machinery was scattered around its half-broken hatch.

"What'd they launch?" Lev muttered.

"Lev, over there! Something fell out!"

Lev glanced toward where Irina pointed, squinting to get a better look. The blankets of flame illuminated two black lumps rolling from the cabin.

"What are those?" Lev had a bad feeling, but he knew he had to find out after coming this far. As he timidly edged closer to the crash, he started to recognize the forms of the black lumps. Poking out from one were shapes like a head and legs nearly burned to a crisp.

"Dogs?!" The realization hit Lev hard; the word tumbled out of him before he was aware that he'd spoken it.

But it was true. The shapes had once been two dogs, and now they were burned nearly beyond recognition, little more than charcoal.

"Eugh!" Crouching, Irina put a hand to her mouth. Her face whitened, and she trembled; her breathing grew ragged, tears welling at the corner of her eyes.

"Irina, are you all right?"

Lev ran to her side, rubbing her back to calm her down, but her trembling didn't cease. Instead, it only grew worse. She seemed to be hyperventilating, and her face was pale, as if all the blood had drained from it.

"Let's get away from here." Lev helped Irina stand, giving her a shoulder to lean on; she couldn't walk on her own.

Just then, they heard vehicles speeding their way. The vehicles encircled the crater at top speed. Delivery Crew members wrapped in black cloaks emerged from within, along with Lt. Gen. Viktor and the army disposal squad. Lev stood at attention under their glares.

"I expect a full report," Lt. Gen. Viktor told him.

Irina was placed in a vehicle to rest, her face gaunt and pale. Beside her, Lev explained everything that had happened before they arrived at the crash landing.

"Understood," replied Lt. Gen. Viktor. "You two can go. Not a word of this to anyone." He turned to leave.

Lev called out to stop him for a moment. "Have you determined the cause of the crash landing? If we can't discern it, that might impact Irina's ability to train."

He made a point of asking the question in front of Irina, knowing her worries would only worsen if they didn't learn the details.

Lt. Gen. Viktor glanced at Irina, then spoke with clear disdain. "The launch was successful, and we have data from orbit. But there were malfunctions during atmospheric re-entry. The angle was wrong, and something happened to the heat shield. That caused a cabin fire, and everything burned."

The biggest hurdle following a launch was successful atmospheric re-entry; the space program had fallen short of that on multiple occasions. Now Irina had seen the price of failure firsthand. Having himself watched a launch fail, Lev understood how that felt; he'd been unable to eat for some time afterward. Knowing at a glance that Irina was incredibly shocked by what she'd just witnessed, all Lev could feel was worry for her well-being.

The entire way back to their cells, Irina sat with her hand to her mouth, eyes downcast and frightened. Lev tried to speak to her several times, but she answered with little more than weak nods.

As they trudged through the red pine forest to the biomedical laboratory, Lev felt a presence in the darkness past the trees. He didn't know whether it was a person or an animal. However, he was focused on Irina's empty expression; at the moment, his priority was to calm her down as soon as possible.

Even after they reached their cells, though, Irina remained completely silent. She headed straight to the shower, avoiding Lev's gaze.

"Damn it," Lev cursed. He wished they hadn't checked out the crash site. He'd never imagined a dog corpse would tumble out of the cabin.

He sat just outside the shower room, trying to think of anything that might cheer Irina up, then heard a pained moan and retching from within.

"Irina..." Lev stood up to knock at the door but stopped himself. If he said something now, she'd only rebuff him with her usual stubbornness.

Irina stayed in the shower some five minutes longer than usual. As she emerged, she hung her head; her hair covered her face, hiding her expression. At the sight of her, Lev was at a loss.

She walked right past Lev, then stopped. "Good night," she said, voice still trembling, and then she went into her room. Her eyes were red and puffy; she'd been crying.

Lev punched the shower door. He hated that he couldn't do anything for her. He felt like a fool for saying he was on her side, only to push her to face such an unbearable situation.

The next day, there were dark circles under Irina's swollen eyes. "Couldn't sleep?" Lev asked.

She was as stubborn as always. "I slept. I slept just fine. But what's with the black circles under *your* eyes?"

Lev had barely slept himself. Worrying about Irina had kept him awake. He wanted to cheer her up, but his mind was completely blank. Saying the wrong thing would just bother her, so he remained mostly silent as the two went out to train.

Irina warmed up and jogged without any issues, although she occasionally let out a deep, heavy sigh. Then they headed for lunch.

Lev had fooled himself into thinking that perhaps Irina's shock at the crash site was just temporary. Its effects were still clear, however. Irina simply sat in place; she didn't touch her food or even her milk.

"What's wrong?" Lev asked.

"Nothing." She picked up the lamb skewer on her plate and bit into it. "Eugh!"

Putting a hand to her mouth as she held back her nausea, she dashed to the bathroom.

"Irina?!" Lev tried to go after her, but she was much too quick. He waited for her to return before saying, "You haven't looked well since yesterday. Are you sure you're all right?"

Irina spat out one of her usual complaints. "It just tasted awful, that's all." But her voice lacked energy, and her face was white as a sheet. In the end, she didn't eat a single thing.

As Lev expected, Irina's state made training even harder. The centrifuge left clammy sweat on her forehead; she looked as though willpower alone had kept her conscious.

"Ah. Now, this is more like it," called Vice-Director Sagalevich. "You look the very picture of a test subject."

His words fell on deaf ears. Irina didn't even have the energy to fire back a retort.

After the hypoxia training, Irina swayed on her feet as if her soul had left her body. Anya—who had no idea what'd happened—watched with fear and apprehension. Since Viktor had ordered Lev to remain quiet, he couldn't even tell her the true reason for Irina's state.

✦ ✦ ✦

Even during their next meal, Irina refused to eat anything; she drank only water. Still, she tried to show Lev she was ready for the rest of the night and morning.

"Today, we're doing parachute training," she said. "Spin recovery, right?"

"Don't be stupid," Lev said, voice harsh. "Spin training's canceled. It'll knock you out cold if you're in bad shape."

Irina shook her head. "I'll be fi—" As soon as she tried to stand, she wobbled precariously.

"Irina!" Lev rushed around the table to her, but he was too late; Irina crumpled to the ground.

"I just...I just slipped," she muttered.

"We're going to the infirmary," Lev said, helping Irina off the ground.

She bit her lip and nodded reluctantly.

According to the doctor, Irina had severe anemia.

She lay on the bed and laughed at herself. "To think that vampires can develop anemia."

Lev thanked and excused the doctor, then turned to speak to Irina alone.

"There's no way you'll get to space if you don't take care of yourself," he told her. "If you really want to fly, you'll tell me the truth."

Irina looked down and eventually spoke. "I couldn't sleep last night because...I was scared. When I think that I might end up just like those dogs, I can't stop shaking, and my head..."

Lev felt heavy. He blamed himself for taking her to see the crash site. It hurt him to see Irina's lips tremble, and to know she'd stayed so strong surrounded by humans who viewed her as simply a guinea pig. Seeing her own potential fate in the dogs' corpses must've shaken her. However hard and tough she acted to protect herself, she was still only seventeen.

"Tomorrow's training is canceled. You need to rest," said Lev.

There was kindness in his voice, and Irina's expression softened a touch.

The next day, however, Irina still wouldn't eat, and she didn't show any sign of recovering when the doctor put her on an IV drip.

"Either human methods don't work on vampires," the doctor said, "or the problem is psychosomatic."

Lev had told Natalia about Irina's poor health; the dorm matron brought warm milk porridge, but Irina barely managed a spoonful before bringing it back up.

There was a faint glint in Natalia's eyes behind her glasses. "If you notice any more changes in her health, let me know right away, all right?" she asked Lev, her voice lower than he was used to. She left with a grave expression.

Irina couldn't sleep long without waking up. Even when she

slept, she moaned as if she was in pain. Lev sat by her side, shoulders slumped.

"I had a dream," Irina told him in a soft voice, her face incredibly pale. "The rocket exploded right after launch. I burned to a crisp, like charcoal. Behind the aurora was hell, and all the scorched animals beckoned me..."

Lev remembered his own launch nightmare. His blood ran cold at the ominous timing of it all.

When Anya arrived with Irina's biomedical test results, she didn't have a pleasant expression. "The numbers look bad," she told Lev. "If Irinyan doesn't get some nutrients, she just won't be able to handle the rest of her training."

"She can't keep any food down," Lev replied.

Irina needed some kind of nutritious, energizing medicine. He wondered whether they could find something.

"Oh..." Suddenly, he remembered Anya telling him about vampires' unique characteristics. "Irina, drinking fresh blood energizes you, doesn't it?"

Irina's reluctant reply was no louder than a whisper. "Yes..."

"In that case, Anya, can you get ahold of any blood-transfusion packs?"

"If we convince the hospital staff of Irina's condition, we might be able to get some there."

"No." The refusal in Irina's voice was clear and decisive. "I'm not letting you put just any human's blood into my body. I wouldn't know where they've been."

"You don't want your blood to be tainted," Lev acknowledged. "All right. What about animal blood, then? Is that fine?"

"I'd rather avoid it, but..." Irina trailed off. "Animals aren't even sold in LAIKA44. The only ones on hand are test subjects."

Lev looked toward Anya. She shook her head quickly. "Dr. Mozhaysky would be furious."

"I thought so," muttered Lev.

Hunting down and bleeding a stray would be pointless—it'd take far too long. What else could they do? Lev was at his wits' end. He held his head in his hands, feeling his pulse through his fingers.

Hang on! An unexpected thought had been hiding under his nose the entire time. Shrugging off his fears, he looked at Irina. "How about my blood, then?"

"Huh?" Words failed Irina; her jaw dropped. Anya reacted the exact same way.

"You can't make a new vampire by drinking someone's blood, can you?" Lev recalled. "In that case, it'll be the same as a blood transfusion. And you know all about me, so it won't be like ingesting some stranger's blood either." His expression was utterly serious.

Irina's eyes darted around nervously. "Er...uh...um..."

"I can't guarantee it'll taste any good," Lev added. "And, uh... the idea of you going for my neck is honestly sort of terrifying, so is my left arm all right?" He started taking off his jacket.

Irina raised her hands to stop him. "W-wait!"

"Hm?"

Embarrassed, she looked away. Her ears reddened. "Are you serious?"

"If there's a chance it'll make you feel better, I want to at least give it a shot. Going to space is your dream, right? I'd like to help it come true," Lev told Irina bluntly, even though Anya was standing there listening.

Irina was silent for a while, thinking. She nodded as if accepting Lev's sincerity. "Then I accept your blood."

"Oh my," said Anya. Being part of the moment had made her feel so awkward that she almost lost her balance as she stood from her chair. "Um, well...uh...I'll wait outside for now, all right?" She left quickly, shutting the door behind her.

Awkward silence wrapped around the young man and the vampire, and the ticking clock echoed throughout the room.

"So, uh...how do we do this?" Lev asked. Taking off his jacket, he offered Irina his left arm timidly. "Should I disinfect the area you'll bite, or...?"

Irina blushed. She played with her hair, looking shy and embarrassed. "I-I'm not sure. You decide."

Seeing her red and uncertain made Lev very bashful himself. "Don't make me decide. Why're you so timid all of a sudden, anyway?"

"I don't know."

Unsure of what else to do, Lev went ahead and rubbed his forearm with a disinfectant wipe.

Irina fidgeted, touching her fangs with both index fingers. "Should I...sharpen my fangs with something?"

"No, it's fine." Sitting on the bedside, Lev held a towel under his arm and moved it toward Irina. "Well..."

"Here goes." She sat up and put her hands to her chest. "My heart's racing," she said, letting out a deep breath.

"That makes two of us." Lev clenched his fist as if a doctor were giving him an injection. He was so nervous, he wondered whether Irina could feel his heartbeat.

Slowly, Irina's head moved closer to the veins rising on Lev's arm. Feeling her breath tickle his skin with slight warmth gave him goosebumps.

"All right, I'm doing it," Irina said. Opening her small mouth as wide as she could, she touched Lev's arm with her fangs and pierced his skin.

"Ngh!"

Lev clenched his teeth, holding back the urge to cry out. He felt dull pain as blood flowed from his body. Irina's tongue licked his arm gently, wet with a mixture of saliva and blood.

After a while, Lev zoned out, the pain melting into sweet comfort. When he looked at Irina's head resting on his arm, his heart and mind were struck with a strange excitement he'd never experienced. Although he hadn't turned into a vampire, tender feelings toward the young vampire woman before him over-whelmed Lev. He lost all self-control and stroked her hair.

"Mm..." Irina twitched and shivered, but she went on sucking his blood.

Lev wasn't sure exactly how much time passed, but Irina eventually lifted her head from his arm. Her lips gleamed voluptuously

with blood and saliva as she wiped her mouth. She looked up at Lev; her eyes were the color of blood, and there was something mature about her expression.

He gulped. Reining in his uncertainty, he spoke—if only because he wasn't sure what would happen to his mind and heart if he remained quiet. "W-was that...enough?"

"It was delicious," Irina said softly, looking a touch embarrassed. Her once-pale face was flushed, and she indeed looked healthier.

"Well, that's good." Lev glanced down at the saliva and blood on his forearm.

Irina rushed to cover his arm with the towel. "Ah! Don't look at that!"

"Sorry!"

Once he'd toweled his arm off, all that remained were two holes, each a few millimeters wide. Lev disinfected and bandaged them like any other minor injury.

Irina finished wiping her mouth and watched him. Feeling her gaze, he turned to her. "Something wrong?"

"Aren't you scared to fly inside a missile that might explode?"

"Of course. But, at the same time, that's a dream worth risking my life for." There wasn't a hint of doubt in Lev's words.

Her eyes widened in shock. "Worth risking your *life* for?"

"If I'm here for any reason at all, it's to visit space. I'd sacrifice it all to get there."

Irina sat up, moving to the corner of the bed. "What makes you feel that way?"

"Well, I have lots of reasons. It's hard to put them all into words. But one thing's certain, and that's *this* feeling." He held a fist to his chest. "It's a desperation to go to space. You feel the same way, right?" He nodded at Irina and then went on. "You were even willing to become a test subject so you could fly. That's no small sacrifice, if you ask me."

"Oh." Irina put a hand over her mouth, surprised.

Lev smiled at her. "The rockets we'll fly in aren't weapons of murder. They carry dreams. That's why they won't explode."

"If my rocket does explode, it'll be because of incompetent human scientists." Irina felt herself pouting at Lev's baseless encouragement. *"Parachute* descent?! How utterly ridiculous."

Lev was glad that Irina was back to her old self. He felt the hint of a smile on his face.

"What're you so happy about?" Irina asked.

"Hmm? Nothing. It's just your imagination." With a wry chuckle, he shrugged off her question and resumed bandaging his arm.

The month went by, and December arrived. It was only twelve days until the newly recovered Irina's launch, and her training had entered its final stages. She kept drilling parachute landings; she'd learned to do solo jumps and touch down without injury, but she still couldn't land in a target area in strong wind. And, of course, they had to do a tandem jump for Irina's spin-recovery training.

"My eyes hurt! Lev! Lev?!"

"Just hang on! You're not the only one suffering!"

"I-I'm going to lose my fingers! My head... It'll split...!"

Upon landing, Irina collapsed to the ground with her parachute still attached. Her face was blank, and her gaze was distant; once again, it was like her soul had left her body completely. As Lev watched her, uncertainty rolled around in his heart. That feeling grew by the day.

Less than a week before Irina returned to training, Lev learned of a shocking decision directly from Lt. Gen. Viktor. During the Nosferatu Project, the launch-rocket cabin's standard survival kit would be replaced with explosives. Lev had been vaguely aware that that choice might be made. It had been the norm during all the dog test launches. The explosives destroyed the rocket or cabin if they crash-landed in foreign territory; the UZSR's higher-ups prioritized technological secrets over test subjects' lives.

In Irina's case, there'd been some debate over whether to load the cabin with explosives. The state commission's verdict was that "However similar vampires may be to humans, the test subject is still a test subject."

On top of that, Irina was much larger than a dog, which would put more strain on the cabin equipment than predicted. The process of refinishing and reinforcing her launch rocket was behind schedule, increasing the likelihood of equipment failure. Irina's chance of safe return had dropped significantly from the original estimate of 50 percent to just above 30 percent.

Korovin himself had opposed loading the explosives, arguing that the launch was a guaranteed success. Given the Parusnyĭ Six's recent crash landing, his words fell on deaf ears. Some committee members had even proposed suspending the space program.

However, First Secretary Gergiev made his decision clear. "If we delay, and the United Kingdom of Arnack beats us to space, then what?! Proceed as per the schedule. What's impossible today, we'll make possible tomorrow!"

The orders to continue Irina's launch and load the cabin with explosives came directly from the government, but Lev still couldn't stand it. Ignoring Irina's safety purely to emerge victorious over the UK was too cruel. If the officials weren't putting the launch on hold, Lev would've preferred that they cancel the project. Then, at least, Irina wouldn't be killed or disposed of.

"Huh?" Lev blurted out, shocked by his own thoughts. Usually, as a cosmonaut candidate, all he wanted was for space program projects to succeed.

Next to him, Irina rubbed her sore eyes after their difficult jump. Looking at her, Lev felt sorrow he couldn't put into words. Irina was no longer a test subject to him but a purehearted young woman and comrade sharing his dreams. He almost couldn't bear the thought of losing her.

However much they struggled, though, Irina's launch was inevitable. Even if Lev helped her escape, she'd eventually be caught, and they'd expel Lev himself from the candidate program. That left him only one option—to do his utmost to support Irina's efforts to achieve her dream of spaceflight.

As Irina got unsteadily to her feet, Lev's voice was no longer uncertain. "We're jumping again. This time, you'll do a standard solo jump."

"Got it. I won't fail." The fierce determination in Irina's eyes pierced Lev's heart deeply.

Six days remained until Irina's launch. When today's training finished, she and Lev would move to the Albinar Cosmodrome so Irina could begin simulated cabin drills in her space suit.

It was their last day of load training, and Irina was being subjected to more pressure than ever before. As Lev watched her spin in the centrifuge, he didn't feel the swell of pride that came from accomplishing something. Instead, his complicated thoughts and emotions formed a weight in his gut.

When Irina's five-minute slot in the centrifuge was over, Lev got ready to check in with her. However, the machine didn't stop. Instead, its motor continued to groan heavily as the centrifuge pushed on to 11 g.

"Hm?" Lev exchanged a glance with Anya. Both realized something wasn't right.

The supervising engineer hit switches repeatedly, looking rattled. Instead of slowing down, though, the centrifuge sped up. Irina's mouth opened and closed as she cried out for help.

The meter showed the centrifuge's gravitational force climb to twelve, then thirteen. 12 g was the upper limit for cosmonaut candidates. At this point, Irina's bones could break and her blood vessels could burst.

Surely an order wasn't given to injure her? Lev thought, glancing at Vice-Director Sagalevich.

Sagalevich stood up, enraged. "What's going on?!" he shouted at the supervising engineer.

Pale, the engineer turned to the vice-director. "I don't know! Something happened to the centrifuge, and it won't stop!"

This wasn't deliberate. Lev panicked.

Anya looked at the data readout, crying, "Her vital signs are dropping! She's blacking out!"

Irina's eyes were shut tight, her brow scrunched in pain.

"Hurry up and stop the centrifuge!" Lev's shout went nowhere.

As if it had transformed into a ruthless torture device, the apparatus continued to spin Irina. If this kept going much longer, her life would truly be in danger.

"Damn it!" Lev shouted. The only way to save her was to destroy the training equipment, he realized. He ran to the switchboard and tore off the cover.

Sagalevich's eyes bulged in surprise, and his voice grew wild. "What do you think you're doing, idiot?!"

"We've got to cut power to the machine!"

"Get back here now, you fool!"

"Stop the centrifuge! Or do you just intend to watch Irina die?!"

"I said get back here immediately!" Even as they argued, the centrifuge's gravitational force was crushing Irina's body.

"Irina!" Lev grasped the cords and wires within the switchboard and tore them out before the furious Sagalevich's eyes.

"You imbecile!"

"It's my job to protect her!" Lev said. He grabbed a steel chair and swung it at the meters and circuit boards, destroying them.

The centrifuge lost power within moments, and the machine came to a halt. Lev and the supervising engineer rushed to check on Irina. She hung limply in her seat, her clothes stained with blood.

"Irina?! Are you all right?!"

Irina looked toward Lev and mustered a hint of a grin. "I'm fine... I'm just...just a little dizzy." She was barely conscious as they laid her on the floor.

"I'll call a doctor!" Anya tripped over her feet as she dashed away.

Although Lev just wanted to make sure Irina could rest, Vice-Director Sagalevich's fury had yet to cool. "You complete, utter fool! Stupid boy! Do you have any idea what you've done?!"

Lev was prepared for some punishment, and he knew it wouldn't be as simple as a fine. As he stood ready for Sagalevich's tirade, however, the vice-director looked down on Irina with hatred.

"And you!" he snarled. "It's because we put your cursed, godforsaken species in this machine that it broke in the first place! Will you apologize with your life?"

The words were too much—too horrid. Lev ground his teeth hard and held back his anger. If he jumped in, he'd only repeat the past. He'd no longer get a simple slap on the wrist, and he'd already destroyed valuable equipment. *But am I supposed to simply stand by and watch this happen in silence?!*

His mind stopped racing as Irina struggled to sit upright, glaring back at Sagalevich. "What're you looking at?" barked the vice-director.

Irina didn't flinch at his anger. Instead, she funneled what energy she had left into her voice. "You really need me to say it? I'm looking at a despicable, pitiful human!"

"You dare speak down to me?!" His voice ice-cold, Sagalevich stomped on Irina's shoulder. Irina cried out, gripping her shoulder as she grimaced in pain.

Lev's thoughts froze at the sight. When he attempted to move in, though, Irina was already shouting back at Sagalevich. "Does your Lord teach violence against others?!"

"Don't you dare speak the Lord's name!" Sagalevich stomped on Irina again, then spat at her. "You're merely walking space debris!"

Lev could no longer stand it. "Shut up!" he shouted, moving toward Sagalevich. "Stop it! Get a hold of yourself!"

Sagalevich choked out a gasp, reeling at the power and rage in Lev's cry. Lev closed the distance between them further, grabbing the crucifix around the vice-director's neck as though he were going to wrench it off completely.

"She's staked her life on a chance to go to space, and you stomp all over her dreams?! Is your God the creator of a heartless scumbag and bully?!"

"You—!"

"You make me ashamed to call myself human! Don't you dare touch her again!"

Overcome by Lev's anger, Sagalevich stepped backward, but he tripped and fell awkwardly onto his rear.

"Ow!" The vice-director rubbed his backside.

Looking down at him, Lev grew louder again. "Apologize to her! Right this instant!"

"Lev! I'm fine!" Irina cried.

The sound brought Lev back to his senses. "Oh..."

He watched Sagalevich climb to his feet, knowing he'd just crossed a line he wouldn't be able to return from. Still, Lev wasn't about to lower himself before this man. He'd done nothing to apologize for.

The vice-director stood and looked down at Lev with demonic fury. He gripped the young man's collar as if to choke him. "I'll see you court-martialed for this." His voice was ice.

Lev didn't turn around to look at Irina, but he felt her sad gaze on his back.

After the centrifuge incident, Lev was taken to the Director's Office in the Training Center without a chance to exchange a single word with Irina. He was to be held in solitary until the military authorities made a decision.

Lev sighed—another of thousands he'd heaved within his cell walls. Irina's launch was now only four days away. The doctor had cleared her as healthy, so the project was proceeding as scheduled. Irina had left for the Albinar Cosmodrome with Anya, Lt. Gen. Viktor, and some others.

Hearing this information from the Delivery Crew member who brought his meals, Lev felt despair wash over him. Now he might never see Irina again; he had reason to think they'd be separated for the rest of their lives. Lt. Gen. Viktor had told Lev that, because the technicians had struggled to lighten the cabin sufficiently in time for Irina's launch, they'd thinned its heat shield. It met the minimum thickness required for launch but lowered the likelihood of Irina's safe return to just 10 percent.

Furthermore, Lev's own dreams of visiting space were now little more than distant memories. However much he apologized, it was already too late. Although he hadn't resorted to violence, he'd again turned on a superior—and this time, it was a vice-director. He would almost certainly be expelled and banished from LAIKA44, and Lev guessed that alone wouldn't be the extent of his punishment.

He sighed again, as if sighs were the only thing his drained body could create. "I wonder if Irina's doing simulation training now."

Lev thought back to his first time seeing inside a rocket cabin. It had felt like stepping onto sacred ground—after all, the cabin connected to the world of the unknown. He'd taken off his cap and shoes reverently before entering, and he'd felt entranced as he peered at the equipment.

"I wonder what a launch feels like."

Lev remembered watching the recording of Maly's launch. At the moment of takeoff, the dog's eyes had widened with surprise. Gravity had pushed Maly backward as the rocket accelerated, but the dog's four legs held strong until the rocket made it to space and zero gravity.

"I wonder if takeoff will feel the same for Irina."

Maly had died after that launch. Would Irina make it back safely? Could she descend by parachute, like they'd practiced? Would they ever have a chance to skate again? Would she be able to keep her promise to share a drink of zhizni on her twentieth birthday?

Rolling up his left sleeve, Lev saw that the holes Irina's fangs had made so she could drink his blood had almost fully healed.

Nobody came to tell Lev his sentence, so time passed slowly in the cell, punctuated only by his constant sighs. He couldn't eat. Nightmares of failed launches plagued him, and his face grew gaunt and weary.

Finally, the launch date—December twelfth—loomed. Lev's watch showed 2300 hours. If everything went according to schedule, Irina's rocket would launch the next morning at 0500. But Lev was stuck in a basement prison far removed from the reaches of space, devoid of even stars. There, Lev's regrets whirled and grew, paining him so badly that he felt as if he were on the brink of tears.

"Damn it!"

Since his pent-up rage had nowhere else to go, Lev sent it through his fist into the floor over and over and over. Still, he believed in his decision to stand up to Sagalevich, even if it meant losing his chance to become a full cosmonaut candidate again. If he'd just stood by and watched Sagalevich hurt Irina, that would've been turning his back on what he believed.

"Irina... Please just make it up there safely."

Then, while Lev stared at his bloody fist, it happened. The sound of boots stopped in front of Lev's cell. Judgment had come.

The door opened before Lev had a chance to prepare himself. Outside were two Delivery Crew members, and behind them, someone wearing a blazer and a cap pulled low. The face under the cap was one Lev knew well.

SCARLET EYES
• ОЧИ АЛЫЙ •

A LAYER OF POWDERY WHITE SNOW covered the endless expanse of rocky desert, and frosty clouds blocked the moon in the dead of night. In summer, this location got as hot as fifty degrees Celsius during daytime, but in December it was a barren place where the temperature never rose above zero.

This desolate spot was the site of the Albinar Cosmodrome, a closed city that took its name from the mines some five hundred kilometers away. The Cosmodrome was equipped with cutting-edge flight data equipment and rocket-launch facilities, each connected to a rail network for delivering supplies. The ground where the recent disaster had occurred was scorched black, and countless carnations decorated a memorial commemorating those lost.

In accommodations on the outskirts of the Cosmodrome, Irina lay in bed, her entire body connected to various machines gathering prelaunch data. Try as she might, she couldn't sleep a wink. In just a few hours, she'd put on her space suit and enter the cabin.

"I'll be in that round part at the top." She sighed, feeling fear and excitement at the idea of stepping into the unknown.

Memories of the launch simulation two days before filled her mind. The cabin itself was an aluminum sphere two and a half meters across, its interior inlaid with rubber and padding. In front of the pilot's seat, which took up most of the cabin, was a panel housing four gauges and a small globe. Compared to a fighter plane, it was very basic.

A cute little stuffed black dragon hung from the cabin ceiling. The occupant would know they'd entered zero gravity when the toy began to float. Around the seat base were the ejection system used during descent, a parachute, and something much more ominous: explosives.

"Try anything suspicious during the test flight, and they'll go off," a Delivery Crew member accompanying Irina had said, seeing the uncertainty on her face.

Irina had no intention of sabotaging the flight, but being reminded of how little her existence meant in this place depressed her. "I really am nothing more than a test subject to these people," she murmured.

Her one self-professed ally, Lev, wasn't here. He'd been thrown into prison over protecting her. The higher-ups had separated them before Irina could say anything to him—no words of gratitude, no apologies, not even a farewell. Since leaving LAIKA44, Irina had been full of regret. Over and over, she wished she'd just taken Sagalevich's abuse, not talked back to him.

When she'd asked Lt. Gen. Viktor about Lev, his reply was curt. "It's not your concern." Even Anya, with a pained expression, had to admit she didn't know anything about Lev's situation.

"Lev..." Irina stared at the stone in her necklace, the lunny kamen.

There was a strong knock at the door, followed by Lt. Gen. Viktor's husky voice. "Wake up. We'll begin on schedule."

It was 0100 hours. Viktor and Anya had come to her room, and now they'd head to the launch area to prepare.

Clad in her uniform, Irina received a "blessing" from a priest in a black robe. He dipped a horsetail brush into a pail and sprinkled holy water on her, praying for God's protection. Not realizing that she was a vampire, the priest conducted the ritual methodically. Irina simply wished the blessing would end—the prayer meant nothing to her.

For some reason, she thought of Lev's kind, warm smile, and sorrow welled up inside her. All she could do for now was hope he was safe.

At 0200, the rollout was proceeding on schedule. Engineers and technicians called back and forth inside the hangar housing the twenty-million-horsepower three-stage rocket engine.

"Loading brake propellant!"

"Loading nitrogen for altitude control!"

Once the cabin had been affixed at the top of the rocket, that section was lowered horizontally onto a train. The engineering team watched as the train slowly left to deliver the section to the launchpad some ten kilometers away. Irina wasn't present for any of this; in the army, it was believed that a pilot watching the rollout was bad luck.

Leaving her accommodations, Irina headed to the production wing to meet with Korovin.

"Private Second Class Irina Luminesk, call sign Lycoris," Korovin said. The call sign was a nod to Irina's scarlet eyes. "Here are the documents you'll need to read in the cabin."

Irina took the sheet of paper from Korovin. On it were two recipes: one for Zirnitran borscht, the other for the UK's cheeseburger.

"In brief, it's just as you were told yesterday," Korovin continued. "After lunch, you aren't to say anything, aside from reading the recipes on that paper. Write down your reports in the flight log."

"Understood."

The Nosferatu Project wasn't just testing zero-gravity conditions; it was also confirming the security of vocal transmissions from space. If the UK tapped into plainspoken communications between Irina and UZSR personnel, they'd suspect that the Zirnitra Union had covertly launched a human into space. Thus, Korovin had suggested that their communications be anything but plainspoken. While a choral tape played inside the cabin, Irina would read a recipe as a coded message.

"If you reach zero gravity safely, read the recipe for borscht," Korovin reminded her. "If anything goes wrong, read the cheeseburger recipe."

"Understood."

Korovin's chest swelled; he couldn't hold back his excitement so close to launch. "Let those hamburger-stuffed fools tap our radios! Let them eavesdrop on our cooking show!"

Unlike him, Irina was more worried than excited. She imagined being in the cabin, looking at the recipes.

Korovin placed his hands on her small shoulders. "Rest easy. If you're worried about the zilant, he'll be here soon."

"Huh?"

Korovin grinned at the confused Irina and then walked off to the launch area.

Irina was dressed in her space suit, and a final inspection ensured that it was airtight. The suit was fitted with equipment to monitor her heart rate, brain waves, blood pressure, and other vitals via radio. It all reinforced the fact that this was a test—an experiment. Irina still couldn't grasp the meaning of the words Korovin had left with.

Just before her helmet was secured, she started to put on her necklace.

An engineer stopped her. "Leave it."

"But...I want to take this with me."

The engineer wasn't about to allow such a breach of the rules. "You can't. No unnecessary items are permitted during the launch."

"But this is necessary to me!"

"You aren't trying to smuggle a bug onto the rocket, are you?!" The engineer reached for the moonstone.

"Stop it!" Irina refused to let the necklace go. "Don't touch me!"

She crouched to protect herself as several more engineers surrounded her. One pried open her hand, pulling the necklace chain free of the jewel. All that remained in Irina's grip now was the lunny kamen itself.

"No!" she cried.

"Give it up!"

"No..." Irina felt tears well in her eyes, then heard footsteps rush close.

"Hold it!"

The voice was immediately familiar and comforting, and the blood flowing through Irina's body rushed to her heart all at once. The engineers surrounding her stepped backward, and there stood Lev, panting a little.

"Lev...?" Irina couldn't believe her eyes. He was supposed to be imprisoned, yet here he was, standing before her. Why?

Lev saw the chain on the ground and caught on quick. He showed the engineers his ID, ducking his head apologetically. "Please, let me handle this! I've been her supervisor since the start of the project."

The engineers glanced at each other and nodded. Telling Lev to hurry up, they busied themselves with other work.

"Wha...? Why are you here?" asked Irina, still perplexed.

"The centrifuge. It was a setup," Lev said, his gaze steady.

"A setup?!"

"Yeah. Natalia told me."

"The lady from the cafeteria?"

"That was just a disguise, actually. She's part of the Delivery Crew."

Irina was lost for words, and Lev went on to tell her what had happened in his cell.

Natalia had appeared before him, clad in a suit he'd never seen her wearing before. Her glasses were gone, and a Delivery Crew badge shone on her collar.

"Natalia...?" Lev had felt flustered, unable to grasp the situation.

"I'm an inspector with the Committee for State Security," Natalia had said, her manner entirely different from the woman

Lev remembered. "I was ordered to surveil the Mechta Project and related initiatives."

"Huh? Then your being the dorm matron in the cafeteria... That was...?"

"I'm tired of playing that country bumpkin—though I suppose it *did* improve my ability to cook." Natalia chuckled. She took an investigation summary from her suit pocket and showed it to Lev. "We've determined that what happened with the centrifuge was no accident. It was caused by the scheming of one specific engineer."

"Who?"

"Someone you know well. Franz Feltsman."

"Franz?!" Lev's jaw dropped.

Natalia went on, expressionless. "He sabotaged the machine to ensure it would malfunction. Have you noticed anything strange in his behavior recently?"

Still reeling from the revelation, Lev thought back to his conversations with Franz. Then it hit him. "When Irina entered the anechoic altitude chamber, he wasn't himself."

Natalia shrugged, shaking her head ruefully. "We tried to keep an eye on you and Irina, but we should've been more scrupulous."

"But why would Franz...?"

"The Mechta Project's failure was likely his goal. His exact motives aren't clear, but we believe one of the Chief's enemies directed him. Feltsman is currently undergoing interrogation, so he's likely confessing as we speak."

Lev was silent, taking it all in.

"You're to forget this incident entirely, Lev Leps," Natalia said.

Although he felt suddenly lost, Lev managed to speak. "Permission to ask a question?"

"Granted."

"What will become of him? Franz?"

Natalia's eyes were icy. "The person you're talking about doesn't exist."

In other words, Franz was now buried in darkness. The UZSR would use its power to erase all photographs and records of the man.

Natalia put the report back in her suit pocket and moved toward Lev. "One last thing. The centrifuge accident never happened, so your actions against a superior *also* never occurred." She took out a new piece of paper—an ID for Lev to access the military airfield.

"Huh?"

Natalia leaned in and whispered in his ear. "You're free to do as you wish."

For a moment, making sure that only Lev could see, she flashed the dorm matron's smile.

"So, I flew here as fast as I could. I can't believe I made it in time!" Lev concluded, smiling brightly.

"I don't recall especially *wanting* you to be here." Although

Irina was delighted to see him again, her words were entirely contrary to her emotions.

"But *I* wanted to come! I wanted to see my understudy's first launch!"

"Since when am I your... Ugh! I'm not even going to bother."

"I assume that means my being here won't bother you!" Lev exclaimed. He pointed to the jewel clasped in Irina's hand. "Look, I know how you feel, but you have to leave it. Want me to ask if there's a safe or something?"

Irina knew the stakes: She might not make it back. If that was her fate, she at least wanted to reach the stars with the lunny kamen. Now, though, she felt she could entrust the jewel to someone special if they were connected by blood.

She held the moonstone out to Lev. "Someday, when it's your turn to fly...bring it with you."

"Huh?"

"You can't?" she asked, second-guessing herself. "Is it because you're a reserve?"

"No, it's not that," Lev said with a laugh. "Look, I'm sorry, but I'm not bringing it with me."

"Oh...all right."

Irina had never imagined Lev would just refuse. She wondered whether it was because she was always so rude to him. Loneliness gouged her chest, and she looked at her feet as Lev spoke.

"I don't have to, because *you* can take it yourself when you go to the moon," he said, his voice warm. "Still, if you want me to hold on to it for now, *that* I can do."

Lev's reply almost stopped Irina's heart. "Oh."

"What? I mean, you *are* scheduled to return around mealtime, right?"

Lev wasn't just trying to be nice. His beautiful indigo eyes shone with unshakable faith that Irina would return. It hit her right in the heart, and it took everything she had to suppress her emotions and reply with her usual venom.

"Of course," she snapped. "I'll be back before you know it. If you even think of selling my moonstone, you'd better watch your neck!"

"I wouldn't dream of selling it," Lev chuckled. He wrapped the jewel in a handkerchief and placed it carefully in his pocket, then called to a nearby engineer. "We're ready to go!"

The engineers came back to fit Irina's helmet. Lev watched with his arms crossed, then clapped his hands as inspiration struck him.

He tapped an engineer's shoulder. "Irina's launch won't be announced to UZSR citizens, will it?"

"No. So?"

"Well, she's parachuting back to Earth in her space suit. Someone might mistake her for a foreign attacker—they might even shoot at her."

"Ah...that *is* a possibility."

"How about we write Zirnitra's name on her helmet? To make it crystal clear that she's with the Union?"

The engineers muttered among themselves for a moment, but they reached a quick decision. "That won't impact the suit's functions, so permission granted."

An engineer handed Lev a black permanent marker. He shook his head. "Best to write it with something more eye-catching."

Grabbing a marker the color of Irina's eyes, Lev wrote "UZSR" in large letters on her helmet. Irina felt a burst of disappointment. *That's not my country!*

As the thought came to mind, Lev spoke just loudly enough that only she heard. "I'm sorry it can't be Lilitto."

Irina's heart leaped at the way he seemingly read her thoughts. "Tell me about it," she muttered, attempting to conceal her feelings. She struggled with this part of herself—the way she was happy about his kindness yet always responded with hostility. She felt lonely when Lev wasn't around but flustered when he was.

"There we go." Lev stepped back to look at Irina.

"You have that dumb grin again," she said.

"Well, the first time you tried that space suit on, it was as though the equipment was wearing you. But now it's like you're a real pilot, bravely flying off to battle on an unknown world."

"It's not *like* I'm a real pilot. I *am* a real pilot."

Lev laughed. "My fault. Of course. You're a full-fledged cosmonaut."

"Yeah."

Irina looked at herself. The space suit was heavy and stuffy, and it wasn't very pretty. Still, she felt proud. Lev couldn't come to space with her, but she felt he was there in the letters on her helmet.

Then Lt. Gen. Viktor's voice boomed. "Time to go! The bus is ready!"

At 0400, the sky was a predawn blue, and the lights around the maintenance tower glowed fantastically bright. Snowflakes covered the ground, and the forecast predicted that the chilly-but-calm wind would pick up after sunrise.

Preparations at the launch site continued. Engineers and technicians bustled like ants around an object that looked like a gleaming silver tower pointed toward the sky.

"The rocket..."

It was the first time Irina had laid eyes on the real thing since arriving. The three-stage rocket was thirty-one meters tall and weighed a total of two hundred and eighty-one tons. Huge metal arms held it in place on all four sides.

"That's what you'll be flying in." Lev's words gave Irina goose-bumps.

"Let's go." The gruff voice belonged to Lt. Gen. Viktor, who pushed them toward the launchpad as if they truly were heading into battle.

Around the launchpad were numerous personages connected to the space program: state commission members, the Delivery Crew's top brass, and Albinar's best researchers and engineers, among others. Korovin, Dr. Mozhaysky, and Anya were also there. First Secretary Gergiev wasn't present, but he'd be expecting a phone call declaring success.

All eyes focused on Viktor, Irina, and Lev's arrival. Lev and Viktor stood at attention and saluted. Irina, too, put her right hand to her temple. But her mouth was a tight line, the weight of silent pressure bearing down on her.

After a second of silence, the chief engineer made an announcement from the blockhouse. "Preparations complete!"

Amid the excited chatter, Lt. Gen. Viktor raised his gravelly voice. "Comrades, the send-off! Take your seats!"

At his command, the crowd sat, then knelt on one knee. A second later...

"Ready for launch!" Viktor cried.

Everyone rose to their feet, giving Irina a long round of applause.

Witnessing the strange, unfathomable scene, Irina felt utterly befuddled. Lev put a hand on her shoulder. "It's a very, very old Zirnitran tradition."

"Does it have some significance?"

"You know, I'm not actually sure."

Irina giggled, her tight expression softening a touch. "Are you kidding?"

Korovin approached the two as they spoke, his piercing eyes on Irina. "You're needed in the cabin, Lycoris. Once you're seated, we'll run the final checks and begin the launch."

"Understood."

Lev put a hand out to her. "Good luck."

"Thanks." Irina gripped his hand in her own; her thick space suit dulled the handshake.

"You'll shake my hand this time, huh?"

"What?"

Lev smiled. "When we first met, you just gave me a glare."

Irina thought back to the way she'd snubbed his greeting. "It was so long ago, I barely remember!"

The launch was approaching slowly but surely. Even now, Irina couldn't bring herself to be straightforward with Lev. Still, the more they talked, the harder it seemed to part with him. She felt ready to burst with emotion.

"I have to go," she said. "So long." Trying to keep her cool, she spun around, turning her back to Lev and entering the lift to the top of the rocket.

"Remember not to panic during your descent! I know you can do it!"

The words came at Irina from behind and stuck fast in her heart. Something warm welled up inside her, and she bit her lip to hold it in. She knew she'd cry if she looked at Lev, so she didn't look back.

The lift rose gradually and steadily. Past the snowy desert, far in the east, the horizon began turning a pale white. Irina's heart palpitated to her extremities, her whole body full of emotion, uncertainty, and excitement. Perhaps this would be her last time on the planet.

"No." Irina shook her head. "I made a promise to come back."

The lift reached the top of the rocket, and Irina walked down the steel stairs to the silver sphere that sat waiting. She bowed once and then entered through the boarding door.

CHAPTER 5

The Territory of the Gods

INDIGO EYES
• ОЧИ ИНДИГО •

AFTER SEEING IRINA OFF, Lev and the others moved to the blockhouse, where the launch orders would be given. A huge concrete horn pointing from atop the building was designed to protect the blockhouse in case of a rocket misfire. There had been many launch explosions, and a vertical trajectory wasn't always guaranteed.

It all reminded Lev of his nightmare of the cabin roof caving in. He quickly shook his head free of the thoughts.

Engineers throughout the blockhouse prepared for the launch quietly and carefully; Lev stood in the corner so as not to get in anyone's way. Irina's face was visible inside the cabin via a monochrome monitor. The picture was grainy and not particularly clear, but Lev could tell she was tense in a way he'd never seen before. Still, there was nothing he could do now but pray for her safety.

Not unlike Irina herself, Korovin was a nervous wreck. He paced back and forth within the room, unable to calm down.

"Polnoc, this is Lycoris." The transmission was from Irina. Regular transmissions were acceptable within the base, since the UK couldn't listen in.

"This is Polnoc. Proceed," Korovin responded.

"Radio transmission test complete. Globe set," Irina reported in a wooden tone, clearly nervous.

"Pulse rate sixty-four, respiration twenty-four. All signs normal," said Mozhaysky, tracking Irina's vitals alongside Anya.

The chief engineer looked at the clock. "One hour to launch." As everyone in the room became aware of that time frame, chatter fell to a bare minimum.

"This is Lycoris. Heart rate normal. Mental state adequate. Launch preparations complete."

The launch time closed in, and the engineers' voices grew more strained with each confirmation.

"Thirty minutes to launch."

"Cabin pressure normal."

Without even realizing it, Lev balled his hands into fists. It felt like an eternity until the launch.

"Ten minutes to launch."

Korovin moved toward the microphone and spoke quickly. "This is Polnoc. Lycoris, we'll launch soon. There will be no countdown. Ignition will follow immediately after a complete system confirmation. Play the choir."

"Understood."

Korovin clapped loudly to bring the room together. "Begin final confirmations!"

The engineers ran their checks.

"Accelerator!"

"Radio!"

"Rangefinder!"

"Launch systems!"

"All systems confirmed normal. Launch on schedule!"

The sound of engineers flicking switches echoed through the room.

Korovin's sharp voice bellowed the next order. "Prepare keys!"

"Preparing keys!" an engineer acknowledged, sliding two keys into the control panel. "Complete!"

"Lycoris, launch is imminent! You may feel uncertain, but there's no need for worry. Believe in the Zirnitra Union's technological might, and believe in us. Be confident and fly!"

"*Understood.*" Beneath Irina's nervous voice, a solemn choir sang over the radio.

Lev hadn't been able to bring himself to tell Irina about the thinned heat shield. All he could do was have faith in the engineering team's blood, sweat, and tears.

"Begin setting the keys!" Korovin shouted.

"Yes, sir!" As the engineers shoved the keys in, the pillars holding the rocket released it.

Korovin barked additional orders. "Ignition switch!" The engineer hit the switch quickly, readying the rocket's first- and second-stage engines. "Preliminary stage!" Rocket fuel burst into flames. "Intermediate stage!" With the launch mere moments away, the air in the control room was tense. "Lycoris, ready for launch! No speaking aside from the recipes!"

"Understood!" On the monitor, Irina bit her lip.

Korovin's passion heated his voice. "Engine ignition! Main combustion! Engine firing!"

As its firepower peaked, the rocket was already trying to leave the ground.

"Launch!" Korovin ordered.

Searing flames fired from the engine. On the grainy monitor, Irina's face was tense.

Images of his nightmare flashed before Lev's eyes. "Fly, damn it, fly." He prayed with his entire body, fists clenched tight.

A deafening roar echoed around them, as if the earth were coming apart. Smoke covered the ground. The rocket shook and slowly rose.

"Come on! Fly!" Lev shouted, willing his prayers into reality.

Flames scorched the earth below, and the rumbling sound of the launch grew louder. The rocket gained speed, its engines unleashing blinding light. It continued to shoot upward, piercing the clouds, and was swallowed by the still-dark sky above. The launch had succeeded.

Lev's hands trembled with excitement. "It's flying!"

Applause and joyous voices filled the control room.

"Yes!"

"Success!"

Korovin cut through the joy, silencing everyone. "Quiet!" he ordered. "This is only the beginning—the rocket has yet to reach space! Those who insist on making noise can do so outside!"

"Yes, sir!" The engineers composed themselves, returning to their duties.

Lev was relieved that the magnetic-tape readouts on the state of the cabin weren't reporting issues. In his pocket, his grip on the lunny kamen tightened, and he prayed the rocket would continue smoothly into space. As the launch echoed in his ears, he listened to the engineers run status checks.

"Altitude is four thousand. Five thousand. Six thousand..."

"Fuel normal."

"Oxygen normal."

"Acceleration rate is 4 g. 5 g."

Everything was proceeding smoothly, but Irina wasn't visible on the monitor—there was too much interference. That made Lev a little nervous, although the video feed had no direct impact on the flight.

"Cabin pressure 13 to 14 PSI. No issues."

"First-stage jettison complete."

"Good!" Korovin exclaimed. "Keep it up!"

As the rocket neared space itself, excitement filled the control room.

"Cabin temperature holding at twenty degrees!"

"Initiating third-stage ignition!"

"Huh? What's this?!" Mozhaysky, who'd been watching the telemetry data carefully, suddenly sounded worried. Nervous chatter filled the room.

"What happened?!" Korovin barked.

Mozhaysky twirled his mustache. "Lycoris's pulse increased to one hundred fifty."

"Is that bad?"

"It's manageable, but the test subject could potentially pass out."

Lev's heart sank. The number on the magnetic tape was at a dangerous level.

Korovin leaned into the microphone. "Lycoris! The recipe!" Even with the radio lines open, there was no response from Irina—only the empty song of the choir. Since the rocket was piloted automatically, its flight would continue smoothly even if Irina had lost consciousness.

Korovin frowned, rapping his forehead in frustration. "Damn it."

"Second-stage jettison complete."

"Nine thousand five hundred. Ten thousand. Eleven thousand."

"Rocket has breached the atmosphere and is now in zero gravity."

"Burn complete."

"Lycoris!" There was no response. Korovin turned on the technician in front of the monitor. "When will that blasted static clear?!"

"We're looking into it!"

A foreboding feeling swelled inside Lev. Had Irina blacked out? Could she still read the recipe?

"Jettison complete. Cabin has entered orbit." The voice of the engineer updating the launch's status sank into gloom. Irina had reached space, but nobody was happy now that they knew she was in some kind of trouble.

Various guesses flew across the room.

"Was she knocked out by excessive g-force?"

"Did zero gravity affect her brain?"

Engineers and technicians bickered over potential issues, but with the display entirely static, there was no way to confirm Irina's status.

The head of the state commission gripped his crucifix. "Lord, we pray for your protection..."

"Lycoris's pulse has dropped to a normal level," said Mozhaysky, but he didn't sound hopeful.

Anya looked out the window, worry written across her face. "Irinyan..." she whispered.

Lev stood still, clasping the lunny kamen tightly. "Please, Irina...say something..." He prayed with everything he had. Then...

"Hm? Where am—huh?!" Irina's shocked voice exclaimed over the choir's continued singing.

Korovin leaped toward the microphone, spit flying as he shouted, "Lycoris, are you safe?!"

"Oh!" It sounded as though Irina had recovered. She began her transmission. *"Um...here's today's Lycoris Cooking Show. Tonight, we'll have...borscht with beets and sour cream."*

"Borscht!"

The engineering team, all of whom were listening closely, whooped with joy.

"First, cut potatoes...and carrots...into bite-sized pieces." Irina's

quiet reading stood in stark contrast to the high spirits in the control room. Her voice sometimes faltered, a clear sign that she was tamping down her feelings. *"While those simmer, prepare the sour cream..."*

With a strange emotion beyond merely "impressed," Lev realized they were hearing Irina's voice from space. "Oh, Irina..."

He pictured her in zero gravity. Was she floating gently in the cabin? What did the planet look like from there? Was the moon clearly visible too?

"Dr. Mozhaysky, how are Lycoris's vitals?!" Korovin cried.

The doctor nodded. "All within normal ranges!"

"Yes! Then we have our first success!"

First, there were sighs of relief. Then, the room erupted into applause, hugs, and handshakes. Even Lt. Gen. Viktor allowed himself a grin. Despite it being a vampire who'd gotten there, reaching space was no small feat, and the room filled with celebration.

"No slacking! Atmospheric re-entry remains!" Clearly, Korovin wanted to warn them against being too optimistic, but his cheeks were flushed red. Even he couldn't hide his happiness.

None of this joy reached Irina, however. *"Add parsley and dill to taste, and there you have it,"* she droned on, as though hosting an actual radio program. *"That concludes our borscht recipe. Next, we have a delicious beverage to share with you all."*

Sudden commotion rippled through the control room.

"Wait, a beverage?"

"Did we give her a beverage recipe?"

Korovin frowned at the unexpected communication. As he heard the Delivery Crew whispering about whether to detonate the cabin explosives, Lev's body froze hard as stone.

"Nastoyka is made by steeping fruits and herbs in zhizni," said Irina.

The words hit Lev in the heart. "Oh...wait," he mumbled sheepishly. It was Lev's favorite drink—the same thing Irina had promised to toast with on her twentieth birthday. Around him, he heard the engineers discuss the "beverage recipe."

"I guess it isn't a problem?"

"Nastoyka *is* one of the flavors of our homeland."

"We recommend silverberries," Irina continued. *"To start, you'll need to prepare cane sugar syrup. As for the secret ingredient, can you guess what it is?"*

"Cotton-thistle honey," whispered Lev.

"It's a spoonful of cotton-thistle honey. Mmm! Delicious."

"You were drunk on your first sip."

"Nastoyka's got quite a kick indeed! Your whole mouth will feel its searing heat."

Lev chuckled. Looking up at the heavens, he closed his eyes, and the sounds around him faded. In his mind's eye, he saw the cabin floating in space.

Irina's voice fell from on high. *"What's the best music to accompany a drink like this, you ask?"*

"It's got to be jazz," murmured Lev. "'My Beloved.'"

"I prefer the song 'My Beloved.'"

"You don't even know the lyrics," Lev said jokingly.

"Careful you don't go skating after a few glasses of nastoyka. You might be in for a fall!"

Irina, the girl more entranced by space than anybody—who'd danced on the ice like a fairy, stared up at the sky by Lev's side, and sung the poem of the moon—was now exploring the world of the unknown.

"Your dream...did it come true?" Lev asked into the sky.

"Maybe I'm a little tipsy myself," Irina continued. *"I feel like I'm floating."*

As he imagined her in zero gravity, something warm filled Lev's heart to the brim.

SCARLET EYES
● ОЧИ АЛЫЙ ●

AT THE END of her radio "cooking show" transmission, Irina heaved a long sigh. "I wonder whether saying all that was all right."

She'd been ordered not to say more than what was on the recipe sheet she received, but she simply had to share her feelings with Lev.

Looking out the window at the blue planet reminded Irina once again that this was no dream. "I'm really here. I made it to space."

She had no memory of breaking through the atmosphere. She'd been conscious enough to make a flight-log entry right after the launch, but then the rocket accelerated. The pressure on her body had gotten worse, dizzying her and pinning her to her seat, and her vision faded. She'd fought to stay conscious, but during the first-stage jettison, she'd felt tremendous pressure—as if her skull were being crushed—and blacked out.

When she'd come to, she was in space. The black dragon toy floated above her, and the force pushing against her body had vanished.

The window cover had come loose at some point, and through the window, Irina saw a planet veiled in transparent blue. The horizon was an arc of shifting tones from navy to indigo, and a rainbow aurora wavered in the vast, open sky. The sight was like a sacred dance celebrating God's blessings.

Irina had been so charmed, she'd forgotten to breathe. At that moment, a thought she'd never expected floated into her mind. *God's in this place—the real God, not the "god" that oppressed my people.* A little while later, transmissions from Albinar had filled her ears, pulling her suddenly back into reality.

She stared at the Earth floating outside the window with great admiration. "That's where I lived. That's where Lev is."

The cabin spun so gently, it was hard to believe it traveled at twenty-eight thousand kilometers an hour. As it rotated, new sights greeted Irina's eyes. She saw clouds cast shadows over deserts, the sea sparkle under rays of sun, great rivers weave through tropical rainforests, and lightning flash from thunderclouds.

The stars were brighter than they'd ever been on Earth. The window was too small for Irina to make out constellations, but those old myths lost their meanings here in the territory of the gods.

"Oh—that's right. My tasks."

Irina couldn't let herself get caught up in admiring the sky; she had work to accomplish. If she didn't meet the required standard, the humans would deem her useless when she returned, and that would cause Lev a lot of trouble.

She drank some space food through a straw so that Zirnitran researchers could learn more about digestion in space. Even away from Earth, space food retained its odd smell and texture. When she went to drink from the water dispenser, the droplets emerged as little floating spheres, colliding with her helmet.

She giggled. "I wonder if Lev could drink this."

Irina imagined the fun they might have experiencing a launch together, and yearning welled up in her heart. The distance and time it took to reach this spot from the base seemed so much shorter than it had taken her to reach the UZSR from her village, yet it also felt much farther off—as though she might never see everyone again.

"I'll be back soon," she murmured. "And I'll make sure that that reserve Lev doesn't hear the end of this."

Collecting herself, she entered more details in the flight log just before sunlight burst through the window. Irina's space suit protected her skin, but the sun still pained her eyes; without a curtain, she had to block it with her hand.

She closed her eyes, and her heartbeat echoed in her chest. Both her pulse and her breathing seemed the same as on Earth. Irina didn't know what effect zero gravity had on the body, but she knew one thing for certain—it had cleansed the stains on her heart.

So many thousands of times, she'd cursed the world, wishing that it—and the humans who controlled it—would disappear. Those dark, gloomy feelings had vanished, however, and she now saw the beautiful blue planet as sacred and precious.

The blinding light against Irina's eyelids abated. She opened her eyes and again gazed out the window. She was flying over the United Kingdom of Arnack; the sunlight hadn't yet reached there. The darkness of night blanketed the region, and house lights spread across the land like gold dust.

As the cabin continued to rotate, the shining, silver-white moon appeared outside the window.

"Wow..."

The moon was so much larger from the window than from the old castle balcony. She could see its surface so vividly.

"Sinus Iridum...? Lacus Somniorum...?" The poem she'd recited so many times once more fell from her lips. "Palus Somni... Oceanus Procellarum..."

Whispering the words, she remembered her childhood. Clasping her mother's hand on the night of the full moon, chanting the poem together as they looked at the stars. Her father holding her tight in a small chamber in the castle, the sound of artillery fire terrifying her.

"Mare Vaporum...Tenerife Massif..." She was full of a past she couldn't return to. Tears welled in her scarlet eyes. "Palus Putredinis, Sinus Fluctus, Promontorium Laplace..."

She reached for her necklace as always but then remembered that she'd left it in Lev's care. "Ah..."

She knew landing on the moon was a dream she couldn't fulfill, so she was prepared to die for a chance to fly into space. She'd agreed to become a test subject to get there before a human beat her. But now, things were different. Irina's hatred of humans had changed after she met Lev. Her own life might soon end, but she truly hoped that might mean Lev himself could go to the moon instead. And she hoped she could wait behind the aurora for the day he arrived.

Nevertheless, she didn't want to die. She wanted to travel to the moon with Lev. She wanted to skate on that icy lake's surface, to drink nastoyka on the day she turned twenty. She wanted to talk about space until the snow itself melted around them.

"Oh, Lev..." Little tears welled up as Irina spoke his name. They pooled, stuck, beneath her eyes.

The flight proceeded smoothly. As the cabin emerged from Earth's shadow, the horizon brightened. The zero-gravity test flight was ending; soon it would be time to return.

Automated systems sprang into action, engaging the reverse thrusters. The cabin slowed and fell from orbit, heading for the most dangerous flight phase—atmospheric re-entry.

As Earth neared, Irina felt heavier. The scenery outside the window changed; a wavering violet seemed to envelope the cabin. Flames.

"It's...burning," she murmured.

Irina found herself feeling restless as the flames blazed. Although she'd been told that the cabin would become a fireball during re-entry, she was struck by the reality of it happening around her.

Suddenly, the shudder of a collision struck the cabin.

"Huh?!" Irina's seat shook. The stars out the window moved sideways, the cabin itself spinning at high speed. "Wait! What... what am I supposed to do?!"

She wanted to do *something*, but she didn't understand the cabin controls. The images and sensations of spin flashed across her mind nightmarishly. Taking deep breaths to calm herself, she felt pain in the center of her skull, as if a dull object had struck her.

Then, she heard the flames scorching the cabin's outer walls. The temperature gauge rose to twenty-one degrees Celsius. Twenty-two. Twenty-three.

"Wait..."

The engineers' decision to thin the heat shield everywhere but the cabin underside was proving a bad one. The cabin continued to fall, wrapped in flames, and the increasing pressure forced Irina back against her seat.

"Ngh!" Her body was growing so heavy she couldn't move, and her space suit was getting humid.

"This is nothing...compared to that idiot Sagalevich's bullying..." Irina tried to cheer herself up, but her voice wavered, and her face grew pale. As her vision swam, the temperature gauge blurred before her eyes. She was sweating buckets, struggling to keep herself conscious as the cabin reached a temperature so hot she thought she might boil.

"Help me...Lev..."

ПОСТЛЮДИЯ

INDIGO EYES
• ОЧИ ИНДИГО •

"Lycoris! Respond!"

"It's no use! Comms are down!" an engineer yelped.

The re-entry phase had caused a comms blackout, and the radio wasn't coming back.

"Cables ruptured! Monitors unresponsive! Antenna appears to be broken!"

Korovin slammed his fist on the desk in front of him, face red. "What else?!"

"Temperature rising! Heat shield compromised! Potential for fire!" The engineers' attempt to lighten the cabin load was coming back to haunt them.

Lev couldn't stand watching what unfolded as they panicked before his eyes. He grabbed the microphone. "Irina, respond!"

"Stop! You aren't to take individual action without permission!"

Lev didn't release the microphone. "Irina!"

Dread continued to swirl within him. Irina was already weak to heat. Could she bear the temperature? Could she successfully descend by parachute? Was the cabin itself even safe? His heart broke as he pictured her struggling on her own up there.

A Delivery Crew member approached the frantic chief engineer. "Where will the cabin land?! If it's heading for foreign territory, we'll have to destroy it!"

"We expect it to land within the UZSR!" the chief engineer's face was pale. "Forty kilometers from here, in the central part of the Palma Plains. Somewhere within a twenty-kilometer radius of north latitude forty-six, east longitude sixty-seven! Expected landing time is 0712!"

Lev's watch read 0634. Dropping the microphone, he ran to Korovin. "Chief! Please give me permission to search for her!" The exclamation was both a request and an order.

Korovin, his face still red, gripped both of Lev's shoulders. "Granted!" He looked around the control room and gave an order to everyone, including Lt. Gen. Viktor. "You heard the man! Prepare for cabin recovery!"

"Understood!"

The breath of Moroz had caused a snowstorm on the Palma Plains. Visibility was limited; the snow made it hard to see more than a couple meters ahead. The sky was full of ominous stratus clouds, so they wouldn't be able to spot the cabin until it neared the ground.

The recovery squad dispatched from Albinar broke into smaller teams. They rushed around the predicted landing area, keeping in touch via radio. In this weather, it was too dangerous to send out a helicopter, so Lev sped through the frost on a military motorcycle. Snowflakes stuck to his goggles, and the cold cut through his coat straight to his bones. He'd left the base mere moments ago, and already his fingers were numbing.

"Irina! Where are you?!" he cried.

The engineers couldn't pinpoint the cabin's exact landing zone; they didn't even know whether Irina had been ejected. It was a dire situation, but Lev refused to give up hope. As he waited for updates over the radio, he kept searching.

"This is the control room! We expect the cabin to land shortly!"

As Lev heard the transmission, the clouds covering the sky parted, and he saw a fireball plummeting down. "The cabin?!"

Lev contacted Albinar immediately. "This is Lev, confirming a sighting of the cabin!"

"Understood!"

"Was Irina ejected?!" he demanded.

"Unknown! Awaiting confirmation!"

At the vague reply, Lev could only grunt. "Irina!" The ball of fire that was the cabin tumbled mercilessly from the sky. "It's falling..."

Crash! The ground rumbled with the explosive landing. If Irina hadn't ejected, she'd be dead upon impact.

"Please tell me you got out in time..." Lev's heart and body shook. He stopped the bike and looked into the sky for a parachute, but he saw nothing more than snow and ice.

"Irina!" he shouted, but his voice was lost in the howl of the blizzard. "Damn it!"

Lev revved the bike and drove off, praying for Irina's safety as he sped toward the crash site.

When he arrived at the site, Lev's eyes widened in shock. The crushed cabin had buried itself in the ground, its once-silver exterior scorched black, its broken parts scattered across the snowy earth. A vision of burning dog corpses flashed through Lev's mind.

"No. It can't be..." Jumping off his bike, Lev neared the cabin. His fears grew with each step as he got close enough to peek through the door.

The explosives inside the cabin had detonated, devastating the interior. Pale, Lev took a closer look. The seat had clearly ejected; there was no sign of Irina.

"She must've gotten out before the explosion, right?" Lev couldn't relax yet, but if Irina had opened her parachute correctly, she had to have landed nearby. "Hang on, Irina! I'll find you! I promise!"

He leaped back on his bike and took off, snow and dirt flying behind him. The frosty wind was strong, but the sun was rising beyond the clouds, and visibility was a little better. Still, the temperature refused to rise with the sun. If Irina had gotten injured or broken a bone, her body heat would drop until she froze to death, however cold-resistant she was.

"This is bad..."

Lev raced without direction through the storm, thinking of Irina. *Did she land safely?*

"She's fine... She has to be!" He was sure of it. She'd practiced so hard. Right now, all he could do was believe in her.

He raced the bike through the plains, looking everywhere. Suddenly, the handlebars and seat shuddered, and the frame itself shook. The front tire had run over a rock hidden under the snow.

"Ah!" The bike slid and spun out; Lev couldn't regain control. "Damn it!"

The vehicle flew through the air along with Lev. He did a five-point landing as best he could, but his right knee took a beating on the rocky ground below. "Ungh!"

The bike fell onto its side, spraying clouds of frost into the air above. Lev crouched, clutching his knee, where his cold-weather clothes were torn and bloodstained.

"This isn't...*that* bad." Gritting his teeth against the pain, he rose to his feet. "She has to be around here somewhere!"

Limping, Lev hefted the bike upright and sat astride it. Just as he was about to start it up again, he got a transmission. *"This is Viktor! Recovery squad members on bikes, cease searching! Return to base immediately!"*

"This is Lev! Why cancel the search?"

"The temperature has dropped to dangerous levels. We'll continue in more appropriate vehicles!"

Lev couldn't stand just leaving Irina here, abandoning her to such extreme cold. "I'm going to keep searching by bike!"

"Damn it, Lev." Lev knew veins were bulging from Viktor's forehead.

Still, he wouldn't back down. "I won't abandon a comrade I fought so hard with!" He refused to follow the order, prepared for whatever punishment might come his way.

"Lev, you're a—"

Korovin's voice entered the transmission, cutting Viktor off. *"Permission granted."*

"Chief?!"

"Do your duty, zilant!"

"Yes, sir!" Lev revved the bike and took off, roaming the barren, snowy plains that seemed to stretch for an eternity. Still, he couldn't locate Irina.

"Irina!" He shouted and shouted, but she didn't reply.

The cold numbed Lev's body, and his consciousness grew hazy. Memories of his two months with Irina flashed before his eyes.

The terrifying vampire he'd expected had turned out to be a cute girl. Lev had kept his distance from her, fearing for his neck, but eventually he'd realized no such threat really existed—only Irina's stubborn arrogance. Even then, her dignity had shone clear as she'd stood tall and proud against the handcuffs and the pain Vice-Director Sagalevich put her through.

It was Irina's fear of heights, the way she'd trembled uncontrollably, that had really taken Lev by surprise. He'd worried about what to do, but Irina fought hard to overcome her fears. When she froze with terror, Lev had taken her hand and pushed her out of the tower himself. He remembered worrying about how light she was and wondering whether she could really handle the training ahead.

Irina's first time drinking soda water had been soon after that, and she'd dropped the cup in shock. Lev chuckled. Around then, he'd started to feel as though Irina were just another human.

They'd flown and parachuted through the night skies. Irina always fought to reach what she aimed for; she never wanted to lose. She hid her tears, putting on a tough front. "She's always so stubborn."

Now, since she'd gotten a trip to the stars, she was ready to throw her own life away. "But it doesn't mean you *have* to die." Pain throbbed through Lev's arm where Irina had sucked his blood. "Irina! Answer me!"

Lev's voice echoed across the plains, growing hoarse. Yet he refused to believe this was how it would end—that he and Irina would never see each other again. "You made it back safe, right? You didn't train so hard just to end up dying?!"

His bike kicked up clouds of frost as he raced around, searching. Then a tiny flash of red entered his field of vision.

"Hm?" Lev wiped snow from his goggles, squinting for a better look. A bright red flower bloomed in the icy plains. "That's..."

There was no mistaking it. He'd written it in red permanent

marker on Irina's helmet himself. "The Zirnitra Union's initials!" Lev practically fell off his bike. Irina had to be there. "Irina!"

He found her collapsed under a snow-covered parachute. She'd managed to at least get her head clear, so he'd been able to spot her helmet.

"Are you all right?!" He took the nearly lifeless Irina in his arms and sat her up. Opening the front of her helmet, he gasped at what he saw. Irina's eyes were closed, her hair was frozen, and ice covered her eyelashes. Her right cheek was bruised, and the color was sapped from her lips. "Irina! Wake up!"

Lev shouted and shook her, but she didn't respond. He took his glove off and put a hand to her cheek, but it was ice-cold. "No! You said you'd come back! You promised!"

Trying to pull the lunny kamen from his pocket, he fumbled; it dropped from his fingers.

"Irina!" Picking the jewel up, Lev placed it in Irina's palm and closed her hand tightly over it. "You promised you'd take this to the moon, right?! You promised we'd celebrate your twentieth birthday together! Wake up!"

Lev touched Irina's lips. "Bite! Drink as much blood as you need!" He pushed his freezing fingers against her fangs, but still, Irina didn't move. "What about skating again? What about listening to jazz? Come on, Irina!" Tears dropped from Lev's eyes and landed on her cheeks. "You can't let our dream end like this!"

"Ugh..." Irina's eyelids fluttered. Then her scarlet eyes slowly opened and looked up at Lev.

His heart jumped. "Irina?!"

She wasn't entirely conscious just yet. "Did I...make it back?"

"You did! You came all the way back from space!"

Her face, still covered in frost, softened with relief. "So, it's not...a dream..."

"It's not. Your nastoyka recipe reached us from space too!"

"Good," Irina replied with a shy smile. "But...why are you crying?"

"I-I'm not. The cold's getting to my eyes. Hang on a sec while I contact the base."

Lev got on the radio to report finding Irina. Korovin gave a loud cheer, saying he'd send assistance immediately.

"Lev, I smell...blood..."

Irina's comment made the pain in Lev's knee flare up. He'd forgotten the injury for a spell, but as he lifted his leg, he saw that it had stained the snow red.

She began, "You—"

"It's nothing serious."

"Always acting tough."

"Look who's talking. Anyhow, let's get you out of that parachute." Grimacing through the pain, Lev moved behind Irina and unclipped her. She remained silent the whole time. "There we go... Done," he said, parachute in hand. "Now we can use this to block the snow while we wait for pickup."

They huddled together. Using the parachute as a tent helped somewhat, but the cold was strong enough that their bodies refused to stop shivering.

"What I'd give for a little zhizni right now," Lev muttered. "I should've brought some."

The pain in his knee was at its worst. He knew he couldn't take another step. He kept speaking; he felt he might pass out from the cold and pain otherwise. "S-so, how was...space? D-did you see...the moon?" His words formed awkwardly through his chattering teeth.

Irina raised her head to look at Lev. "I..."

"Hm?"

"I heard your voice," she said. "The cabin was hot. I was in pain, and I couldn't move... I thought I was dead. I was ready to give up. Then...I remembered the helmet." Tears welled in her eyes and ran down her face, stopping on her frozen cheeks. "I heard you call to me... I heard it! You told me I could do it...all on my own. You said I'd be fine...doing a solo jump."

She reached up to brush tears from her face, but between her helmet and thick space suit gloves, she couldn't.

"Irina..." Lev reached toward her to wipe the tears, but she stopped him.

"I'm not crying... It's the snow melting. It's your fault for thawing it."

She was too adorable, playing tough as she sobbed. Lev wrapped her in a hug.

"Ah..." For a moment, Irina's body tensed, but then she gave in, burying her head in Lev's chest.

Lev felt the warmth of life behind her space suit's thick layers. He was glad she was back. Right now, that was all he wanted her to know. "Welcome home, Irina."

The truly incredible, groundbreaking task she'd accomplished that day would, perhaps, be forever unknown. She wouldn't be showered in praise, and her name wouldn't go down in history. Perhaps she'd never defy the merciless hand she'd been dealt, and her very existence would be buried in shadow.

But the truth would never change. Irina was history's first-ever cosmonaut.

"I'm here," she said.

Afterword

VOLUME 1 OF *Irina: The Vampire Cosmonaut* is based on actual Space Race events that took place in the 1960s before humans went to space. I modeled the characters on quite a few real people.

Although I aimed to remain faithful to history in this story, I only used it as a foundation while writing. That allowed me to play with characters' ages, include female candidates, and change details about technologies, subterfuges, and conspiracies. (So please, don't go telling me that the plot doesn't match what actually happened.)

There are lots of fictional additions in *Irina*, but the real national secrecy during that time period supposedly created a kind of fiction of its own. I say "kind of" because not only is contemporary documentation limited, but the information distributed at the time often differed from fact...which is typical when it comes to national secrecy. Some people were even erased from commemorative photos because they were considered inconvenient...

By the way, the famous, tragic dog Laika shouldn't be mistaken for a vampire. Laika's in this story under a different name. There's a real inspiration for the vampires too, but the most important part is that vampires aren't humans.

Irina: The Vampire Cosmonaut originated when it occurred to me that there were no fantasy stories in which characters made a conscious effort to send rockets to space. However, when it became clear to me that characters in a fantasy story could never reach space, I rejected that idea. As I brainstormed further, I thought up a postapocalyptic wasteland—like one in a Western video game—where the church was hiding an ancient spaceship. (I still think that's a fun idea.) Then I wanted to write about a time and place authors hadn't really touched until now, and the story took its current shape.

Our century has been called the Universal Century, and long stays aboard the International Space Station are now fairly common. Only fifty years ago, though, the very idea of getting to space was something of a miracle. So if you enjoyed this story about two young people living in that very era and dreaming of space travel, I'm really glad.

Many thanks to my editor, Tabata, for such detailed direction. Thanks also to Karei, who helped bring both the cute Irina and the draconian military characters to life. I'm using her cover image draft of Lev and Irina sitting back-to-back as my PC wallpaper. I've also got nothing but the utmost respect and gratitude to all the people—past and present—who've worked to push space development ever forward.

Thanks so much for reading this volume. For now, I leave you hoping Lev and Irina's dream will come true.

—KEISUKE MAKINO

✦FROM THE AUTHOR✦
Keisuke Makino

In addition to light novels, I write for games and TV dramas. Recently, I worked on the writing team for *Persona 5*. I've developed an interest in Russian cuisine while penning *Irina*, so now I'm craving blini (crepes?).

BOOKS BY KEISUKE MAKINO
Flick & Break
Flick & Break, Vol. 2
Flick & Break, Vol. 3
Irina: The Vampire Cosmonaut

✦FROM THE ARTIST✦
KAREI

I work better at night, so I've been living like a vampire, waking up at night and going to bed in the morning. Thanks to that, I'm as weak as they come.

PIXIV: 3410642   TWITTER: @flat_fish_